STO

THE THREE PEBBLES

The Three Pebbles
by
RICHARD PARKER

Illustrated by
William Ferguson

DAVID McKAY COMPANY, INC.

Copyright © 1956 by David McKay Company, Inc.

All rights reserved. Manufactured in the
United States of America.

Library of Congress Catalog Card No. 56-7959

Manufactured in the United States of America
Van Rees Press • New York

CONTENTS

One:	Gathering the Pebbles	1
Two:	The Indians	36
Three:	The Fort	77
Four:	Farming	108
Five:	Mutiny	135
Six:	Starvation	166
Seven:	The End	207
Historical Note		217

Chapter One

GATHERING THE PEBBLES

THERE WERE three of us to begin with: Pierre Gambi, Pierre the Red and myself. Later we were called the Three Pebbles, which was meant as a sort of joke.

No doubt the full story of this expedition will one day find its way into the history books where it will be mixed up with the doings of kings and queens, great princes and nobles. I know very little about kings and such, however, and for me the story begins with the first meeting of the three Pierres. This was on the 1st May, 1564, in the town of Le Havre on the coast of France. I shall start the story there.

2

I myself had been living in Le Havre for a month by this time. I had no idea what the town looked like for I had crept in, a fugitive, late one night and had spent all the time since either working at the printing press in Mr. Lebrun's cellar, or sleeping on a heap of straw under the type cases in the corner. There were three skylights which I had to keep clean if I wanted any light at all for my work, and when I climbed up to them I could see the sky and the sun and bits of the gables and chimneys of a few nearby houses.

Mr. Lebrun and his wife were very kind to me. Above the cellar they kept a sort of combined inn and shop. Mrs. Lebrun sold vegetables, flour, spices, eggs and so on while Mr. Lebrun served wine to customers who sat outside in the street on long wooden benches. There was always a lot of talk and noise up there which drowned the squeaks, thumps and groans of the old printing press in the cellar.

*Upstairs, then, the Lebruns were respectable business folk; down in the cellar they were criminals, breaking the law of France and defying the King himself. Or at least, I was doing it for them.

I was printing Bibles in the French language, which was a very great crime indeed. Things have changed now, but in those days the Bible was in Latin and was read only by the priests. Anyone translating the Bible into French was a criminal, and anyone reading such a translation was also a criminal. If you tried to make up your own mind what the Bible meant, then you were worse than a criminal, you were a heretic, and you might be burned alive on a great fire of sticks in the market place.

Many people were burned alive in France in those days. Sometimes whole villages were destroyed and all the people in them killed. This happened once in the south of France when I was a baby. I cannot remember it but my father often told me about it.

The village was surrounded by soldiers who drove all the people into their houses. These houses were made of mud and straw and wood and when the soldiers set fire to them they burned easily. In a few minutes, my father said, the village was a great roaring, crackling furnace, with blazing roofs falling in, people screaming and trying to escape and the soldiers in a ring outside the village killing everyone that tried to get past them. I am very glad I was too small to remember anything of it.

My mother and my two brothers were killed, but somehow my father escaped. He wrapped me up in a wet sack and ran through the streets with me in his arms. He says his clothes were on fire and he looked like a human torch as he ran. The soldiers tried to stop him at first, but then one shouted out, "Let the fellow go; he won't run far like that!" And they laughed and let my father through. They thought he would die of his burns, I suppose.

They were wrong. Somehow or other he escaped and got to Lyons, which is a large town and therefore easy to hide in. Later when I was old enough to remember anything at all he had set up a printing press there and was doing a good trade. He had to lead a double life. Most of the time he was working like an ordinary printer, but secretly he was printing little pamphlets, telling about Calvin, a priest who had broken with the Church and run away to Geneva.

When I was about ten or eleven the authorities found out where my father was hiding. A friendly soldier warned him in time and he escaped before they came to fetch him. He got away to Switzerland and so to Geneva where he was safe. I was too big to be wrapped in a sack this time, and as we should have been more easily caught if we had traveled together, I stayed behind with friends.

Later these friends became worried that they were falling under suspicion, so they sent me off to Le Havre with a note to Mr. Lebrun. So there I was in Le Havre, working a secret printing press and living underground like a hunted fox.

It was not a very gay sort of life. I never saw anyone but Mr. Lebrun and his wife and I never got into the open air. After a month of it, my skin was whiter than the paper I used for printing. My eyes hurt often, my head ached almost all the time and I felt I was growing steadily weaker. I decided that I must have a run out of doors whatever the risk.

I decided that the first day of May would be the best and the least risky time to go. The first of May was a holiday; everyone dressed up and danced in the streets and had parties. Many people came in from the country and the town would be so full of strangers that I should never be noticed. Anyway, I hoped so.

On the previous evening I loosened the frame of one of the skylights so that a single push would be enough to raise it, then went to sleep very early in order to be fresh and awake by sunrise.

3

I awoke while it was still dark and with no idea of the time. The patch of sky above me showed an uncertain gray, but it had turned a deep red by the time I had crawled through into the open. I stood for a few seconds taking the first deep breaths of fresh morning air and then made off at a trot through the empty cobbled streets. I knew what I wanted first: a dip in the sea to wash off a month's cellar grime.

The streets were bewildering and I had no idea which way to turn but eventually, because all roads in Le Havre lead there, I arrived at the harbor. I really wanted a deserted strip of beach outside the town, but this would have to do, for I was quite exhausted with running.

The sun had come up and was clearing away a faint sea mist. Half a dozen ships, two anchored in the middle of the harbor and the others tied up at quays, seemed sharp-edged; each rope and seam and bolt clear and appearing almost within reach. In a few minutes I was in the water, looking up at the sun as I floated and feeling the dirt and dinginess peel off me and my skin come alive. To think of the last month in that cellar was to think of black beetles and slugs and pale things that live under stones. I kicked my feet into the air and drove myself so deep in the water that I lost my breath and came up again choking and spluttering.

"God made fishes with tails and fins, but man with arms and legs," said a voice over my head. The words cracked across the water like the breaking of dried sticks, and I looked up to see where they came from. A man in black, dressed half like a priest and half like a soldier, stood on the quay staring down at me. He had on a short, sleeveless leather jacket that shone in the sun as if it had been soaked in oil, and below that he seemed to be all legs: long spidery legs that did not go quite straight and that were far too thin. His stockings sagged like gloomy garlands all the way down to his ankles.

"Leave your shamefulness," he said dryly. "Put your clothes on you and go dressed and upright like a man."

I wanted to shout back something cheeky and rude to the interfering old spider, poke my tongue out or splash him with cold water; but I needed to make myself as little noticed as possible so I swallowed the insults I had all ready on my tongue and swam rather sulkily to the stone steps on which I had left my clothes. The man waited until I had reached them and then walked on.

I was still getting over my irritation at having my swim spoilt when I discovered that my clothes had gone. I looked along the wall to see if I had mistaken the steps, but there were no others near, and in any case I had already recognized a rusty iron ring let into the wall with a distinctive splodge of red seaweed about a foot below it. They were certainly the same steps. I wondered if the tide had risen and floated the clothes off, but in fact the tide was falling, as the wet steps above water-level showed. I looked all around in a hopeless rage: at the harbor, the ships, the wall, and then the steps again, and then I almost fell back into the sea with surprise. For my clothes were there, only six or eight steps higher than I had left them, and squatting on top of them, grinning with delight at the shock he had given me, was a boy of about my own size.

"Thought you'd lost them, I suppose," he said. "Thought some thief had made off with your stuff and left you to dance around in your skin, eh?"

He spoke French in a way I found hard to understand; fast and clipped as if he were in a hurry to finish before someone interrupted him. In the rush he left most of the consonants behind so that the words ran into one another like sweets you have put in your pocket and forgotten. I guessed he came from Paris, and I guessed right.

"Thank you for looking after them," I said sarcastically. "I'm sure if they'd tried to run away, you would have stopped them."

"S'right, old man," he said. "Just thought I'd better stay and keep an eye on them for you."

I climbed the steps and waited for him to move but he continued to sit where he was, very comfortable it seemed and looking up at me with bright, twinkling eyes. He was a queer chap. His head was very small, and his face out of shape and twisted like the little heads you sometimes see carved on the ends of church pews. His hair was brown and short, and it curled all over his head in tight little screws. The clothes he wore, although rather grubby, were of the brightest possible colors: orange jacket, vest of white and purple stripes, yellow stockings and crimson shoes with large showy buckles four inches across. He looked rather like a monkey dressed in a parrot's feathers. I smiled at him in spite of my annoyance.

"Ah, that's better," he said. "A bit more cheerful. You looked like a bishop with the bellyache before. That's more like, that is."

I was willing to be friends. "What's your name?" I asked.

"Pierre Gambi," he said, and then cocked his head on one side as if to watch the effect. "No? You must be a stranger around here, if you've never heard of Pierre Gambi."

"I'm Pierre, too," I said. "Pierre Debré."

"I know you," he said contemptuously. "You've been

hiding away in old Lebrun's cellar for the last month. One of these heretics, you are. What do they call you—have-a-goes or something...?"

"Huguenots," I said. "But how did you...?"

"Thought you'd slip out sooner or later," the other went on. "I was just beginning to think you'd curled up and died down there. Or else that old Mrs. Lebrun had done you in and put you in those meat pies she sells."

I laughed. "Mrs. Lebrun has been very kind to me."

"Ah, I daresay. So she ought to be. They're making a nice thing out of you, they are. All that printing they're getting done for nothing—"

"Not so loud," I said, looking round quickly. "I don't know how it is you've got all this information, but if it spread...."

"As I was saying," Gambi went on, even raising his voice a little, "all that printing for nothing. For they don't pay you, now do they? Own up!"

"As a matter of fact, they do," I began.

Pierre Gambi jumped off my clothes with a broad grin. "Well, that's a relief, anyway," he said. "I had a good look through your clothes and couldn't find a single franc. But as they do pay you, it'll be all right."

"What will be all right?" I asked. "And I must say you've got a nerve searching in my clothes like that."

He smiled a queer, secret smile, letting his eyelids droop down until his eyes were almost hidden. It gave him a strangely old expression.

"Well!" I said. I was almost too angry to speak.

"Yes," he said coolly. "As long as you've got money, I'm not wasting my time. You can pay me when I see you again."

"Pay you?" I exclaimed. "Why should I pay you? For sitting on my clothes, I suppose."

"A hundred francs," he said thoughtfully. "I think that would do—for a start, anyway. And now you come to mention your clothes, hadn't you better put them on? Can't have you catching cold, you know. Not while you owe me a hundred francs."

"But I *don't* owe you a hundred francs," I said. I felt in one way that it must all be a silly dream or a rather long-drawn-out joke, and yet at the same time I knew that it was real.

"Now listen, stupid," the boy snapped in a very different voice, "we've had enough of this, see? You pay me a hundred whether you like it or not. And if you're not quite bright enough to see why, I'll explain it to you in easy stages. Now, first, when I knew you were hiding away in that cellar I didn't go running to the authorities, did I? I might have made something out of it, too. They would have been pleased to know where a certain shivering little heretic was hiding."

"I'm not shivering," I said. "Or at least, if I am, it's because I'm cold."

"Put your clothes on, stupid. I told you once, didn't I?"

I began to dress. "All right," I said. "So you didn't betray me. What about it?"

"What about it?" Gambi spread his arms out wide and looked up at the sun as if asking the answer from there. "I've met them simple before," he went on, "but to be as simple as you are is too good to be true. You ought to be framed in gold and hung up in a church, you should. Now, listen, will you? I didn't tell on you when I might have, see? That means I'm protecting you, doesn't it?

I'm your protector, your bodyguard, your nursemaid, see? You don't think I do all that for nothing, do you?"

"But I don't want protecting," I said. "I can look after myself."

"You're not going to get a chance," said Gambi. "I'm considering myself appointed."

"I shan't pay you."

He looked at me for quite a long time, his head on one side and his eyes almost closed. He looked very like a monkey: an old, experienced, clever and rather wicked monkey. "I see," he said at last. Then he turned lightly away and added in quite a cheerful voice, "I wonder if you noticed a fellow in black a little while ago? Rather on the gloomy side."

"He went along the quay," I said. "What do you want with him?"

"I know him. He's one of the court officials attached to the Inquisition. If I ran, I might catch him up." He was up the steps and a few yards along the quay before I could speak.

"Don't!" I cried out miserably. "Don't go. Perhaps I was wrong. Perhaps I do need a . . . protector."

Gambi came back with a broad, infectious smile nearly splitting his face. "Now you're talking," he said. "I can see we're going to get along very well together." He leaned down and patted me on the shoulder. "From now on, my dear stupid," he said, "consider yourself protected."

4

So there were two of the pebbles and the way they met. From this first meeting, you cannot help but get a bad impression of Pierre Gambi. Of course, he was as I have described him, sharp, clever, unscrupulous and vain. He lived by his wits and could pick a pocket or blackmail a duke with equal skill and self-possession. He knew everything about everybody and turned his knowledge into money. He had no pride and no morals. And yet, when I got to know him better, I discovered much about him that was likable. As you will see, he was always cheerful and gay in the worst circumstances. His humor never left him, and I don't think I ever heard him grumble. He had an immense belief in his own ability and would never sit down and let things happen to him. There were many times when I was grateful to him for keeping me going and laughing me out of sadness and depression. So, although I shall not try to hide his black side—his complete lack of honesty or morals, the hurt he frequently did to others—yet at the same time he was always a good companion to us, and we should not have got very far without him.

Gambi was an orphan, he told me. He did not remember either his father or his mother, and his earliest memories of Paris were of creeping homeless around the streets fighting with other waifs for the dirty crusts, bones and fruit peelings that they found in the gutter. He had seen many die of starvation.

He was older than I was, being fifteen or sixteen when I met him. He said he was a hundred years older, and in some ways he was. On the other hand he could not read or write and respected my learning in this matter. Of course, not many people could read anyway, and it was only because my father was a printer that I had the art.

After our meeting at the harbor that morning, he stuck close to me all day.

"I've got to keep my eye on you," he said. "Can't have you getting caught, you know. You're my next month's meat and drink. Now come on, where would you like to go? I'll show you the sights. You could have no one better."

"I want sunshine and green fields," I said. "And fresh air."

His face dropped as if I had suggested that we boil ourselves in oil. "All cheap enough," he admitted. "But a little of that stuff goes a long way. Still, if that's what you want . . . come on!"

He took me out of town, and for a few hours we wandered about the fields and the dry rutted tracks of the country just behind the town. Now and then he would disappear for a few minutes, first telling me to sit still and wait for him, and then return with fresh bread and wine or a piece of cooked meat. Once he brought a chicken which we plucked and then roasted over a friendly blacksmith's forge fire. Then, as the sun was going down, he stopped a cart rumbling slowly along towards the town and got us a lift. We slept in the straw until the jolting of the wheels on the cobbles woke us in the streets of Le Havre.

"Now the day really begins," said Gambi as soon as his feet felt the hard paving. "First, roasted eels and mulled wine, and then I'll show you another world. My world," he added.

He set off at a half-trot, twisting and turning down narrow alleyways, up steps, in and out of queer shadowy places so quickly that I had lost all sense of direction two minutes after we had started. All I saw was a whirl of lights and faces, open doorways and crowded streets. The air was thick with smells and sounds that changed sharply as we went: wood smoke and broiling sausage, rotting garbage and the sharp reek of garlic, women's laughter, a scream of pain, a baby crying somewhere in the dark, wine, wood smoke again, an omelet of fresh eggs being burnt while a woman laughed in a doorway, all spun round me like a circling nightmare. Then they vanished, and we were standing still.

"The best roasted eels in France," said Gambi, running his tongue round the front of his teeth and pushing his lips out to look more like a monkey than ever.

We were in a dark, circular courtyard with scrubbed, gleaming stones underfoot, not cobbles but the rounded stones of the beach that rolled and gave off warning as you walked on them. Nets, lobster pots and long, sleeve-like eel traps were stacked all around against the walls except where a big stone tank of water was set in the ground. In the center of the court was a large iron brazier filled with glowing blocks of wood, and around the brazier, though drawn well back out of respect for the heat, were people sitting in a broken circle. Some of them ate from large wooden bowls, some held pewter flagons which they kept raising to their lips.

An elderly man and a plump young woman who might have been his daughter went continually between the fire and the water tank. I saw the man plunge his hand into the water tank and fetch out a small eel a foot or so long which curled round his wrist and wriggled, shining, in the firelight. With what seemed like one continuous movement of his knife, the man beheaded the eel, skinned and gutted it and then came to the fire, spitting the creature in loops on a thin steel spike. He hung the eel somehow against the side of the brazier, shielding his face from the great heat with his apron, and then went back to the tank.

The girl looked up when our feet clattered on the loose stones, screwing her eyes up to look out from the glare of the fire. "Pierre!" she cried, pleased. "So you have come. We'd given you up for lost this time."

"We thought your sins had found you out," shouted a short, red-faced man from the circle. "It's about time they did."

"No," said the girl. "Pierre is no common thief. He robs the rich to help the poor, don't you, Pierre?"

"What poor does he help?" demanded the red-faced man. "I've never seen him at it."

"He spends most of his earnings with us," said the eel man, "and everyone knows that we are poor. Pierre is a humanitarian."

Pierre swaggered towards the fire, pleased with his welcome. Standing with his feet wide apart and his hands on his hips, he looked calmly round at the circle of faces. He looked like a jay surveying his drab cousins the rooks.

"My friend and I have just passed the day in the country," he announced. The eyes flicked towards me for a moment and then lost interest and returned to Pierre. "And we have made several important discoveries," he went on.

"Such as, pigs don't fly?" shouted someone.

Pierre raised one hand with absurd dignity. When there was silence he said in a low, solemn voice, "How many of you knew that milk does not grow naturally in buckets at all. It comes from a large grass-eating creature known as a cow?"

"Truly amazing," said the eel man with pretended seriousness. "Such travelers' tales are hard for us simple townsfolk to believe."

Among the general laughter and friendliness, I found myself sitting down, a little bewildered, on one of the lobster pots that acted as chairs, grasping a flagon of wine in my hand and with a bowl of steaming roast eel in my lap. I raised the flagon to my lips to taste the wine.

"Wait!" cried my neighbor catching my arm before I could drink. "Look! Like this!" He went to the brazier and drew out a sort of poker with a curved wooden handle. The iron tip was almost straw colored with the heat and winked and glimmered on its surface with tiny sparks. He held it for a minute or so until the heat had sunk to a dull red glow and then plunged the hot end into my flagon. Immediately the wine foamed and bubbled and threw off a great cloud of pungent steam.

"Now it's mulled," said my new friend. "Taste! This wine is not good enough to drink any other way, but when it is mulled it is quite passable."

I thanked him and tasted the wine. The warmth and the faint taste of scorching were certainly rather pleasant.

"Be careful, though," he added. "It goes more quickly to your head that way."

As I drank, I inspected my neighbor over the rim of my flagon. He was a sturdily built fellow of about seventeen, not above average height, but with an unusual width of shoulder. He looked as if he might be very strong. His chest was well developed and the muscles at the sides of his neck were so heavy that they made his shoulders appear to slope. He had bright red hair which he wore cropped very close, almost shaved at the sides and back. On top it stood up like stubble stalks, but more evenly cut. He was tanned by the sun and looked like a countryman. I liked the look of him straight away, especially his very bright blue eyes and fair eyebrows bleached almost white by the sun. I imagined that they showed honesty.

After a while he saw me looking at him and gave a large, easy smile. "What is it, friend?" he asked. "Have we met before?"

"I don't think so," I said, a little confused. "I was staring rather rudely, I'm afraid. I'm sorry if I offended you."

"Offended?" He laughed. "Nonsense. Where I come from we are not afraid to look at one another. It's a townsman's habit to peek at people's waistcoats and over their shoulders. But then, you're not from here, either, are you?"

"No," I said. "But how could you guess?"

"I don't know. You're pale enough for a town dweller. It's just a feeling I have. What is your name?"

"Pierre Debré," I said.

"Mine's Pierre, too, though I'm not usually called by it. Mostly people call me Red, for obvious reasons. What about this bright fellow you came along with. Is he a friend of yours?"

"We met this morning," I said, sticking to the bare truth.

Gambi sensed immediately that he was being talked

about and he broke off his conversation with the eel man's daughter, strolled casually over to us and sat down at my other side.

"You've been fixed up with food and drink, then?" he said to me. "Making yourself quite at home, eh?" He glanced at my red-haired neighbor inquiringly as he said this so I introduced them.

They were both a little on edge for a few minutes, stiff and formal and apparently trying not to like each other, but then Red's fundamental friendliness began to break through. Gambi on the other hand could not sustain any mood for very long, and in a very short time all three of us were laughing and joking together like old friends.

Then, in the middle of it all, there came a sudden silence. Everyone in that little courtyard stopped speaking at the same moment as if the air had turned suddenly to water. Red was laughing heartily at some comic story of Gambi's and his laughter went hurtling round the walls like an exuberant monkey against the bars of its cage. The faces in the firelight all stared together in one direction, all rigid as if carved, and the only movement was that of the shadows on their faces, shifting with the fire and giving new expressions to everyone.

"Good evening, friends," said a voice behind us, and then footsteps advanced across the stones. Both voice and stones made the same dry, mechanical sound, and I knew what I should see before I turned my head. It was the man in black with the spidery legs who had called to me that morning in the harbor.

Although I had no reason to suppose that he suspected me, yet I felt an unpleasant chill creeping down my back. The others must have felt much the same thing, for although they turned back to their conversation as soon as the stranger had been greeted, not one of them lifted his voice above a murmur. The cheerful gathering around the brazier had been spoilt.

The stranger himself did not seem at all perturbed by the obvious effect he was having. He went close to the brazier and held his hands out to the heat, looking round the circle as he did so, face by face, as if he were running through a handful of coins to see if he could find any counterfeit there. Some of the men tried to stare back at him, but most of them dropped their eyes first. Others gave him a fleeting glance and then concentrated nervously on their wooden bowls.

"You are keeping the fire off us, master. Be so good as to move aside a little!" The voice, clear and strong and unafraid, was Red's. It was greeted by a little hissing noise that ran quickly round the circle as all there took in a sharp breath of surprise.

The man swung slowly round to stare over his shoulder at us. His face was wooden and expressionless, and against the fire his ears seemed thin as paper and showed the red light through. Still staring he moved a yard or so to one side so that the firelight fell directly on to us again.

"Thank you," said Red, and bent to pick up his flagon as if dismissing both the man and the incident.

"You must excuse an old man," said the stranger, every word snapping like a whiplash across the back of the silence. "I have a reputation for being very fond of the fire."

Considering the man's occupation as an employee of the Inquisition there was a grisly humor to this statement that did not escape the crowd there. Again there was the faint hiss of intaken breath, and then utter silence.

Red, however, was inspecting his wine with concern and paid no further attention to the grim stranger. "Ah, I thought so," he said into the silence. "Some ash has fallen into my flagon."

I mumbled something about having a spoon with me, as indeed I had, and began to search hurriedly in my pouch for it. As I drew it out triumphantly, I also pulled out with it a piece of folded paper which fluttered towards the fire and dropped on the ground a few inches from the stranger's right foot. He bent and recovered it and was about to hand it to me when his eye caught half a word of print and he drew his hand back and began to unfold the paper.

Straightway I remembered what it was. It was a galley proof of the last page of type I had set up the day before—the beginning of the first chapter of the Gospel of St. John. My blood seemed to drain out of me leaving me weak and helpless, then flooded back so that I began to rise to my feet in a sort of panic, ready to run away.

At this point Red put his large hand on my arm and pushed me firmly down in my seat. "Your wine is cold," he said in a normal, friendly voice. "Let me warm it for you."

I sat perfectly still and watched the man in black. He had opened the paper now but was having difficulty reading it. He bent down, holding the paper low so that the firelight shone on it. I could see his inverted face with dark shadows under the bony jaw and the straight ruled line of his brows. He frowned more heavily and grunted to himself as if he had suddenly realized what it was he read.

Meanwhile Red went to the brazier and drew out a hot mulling iron. As he turned back his foot slipped on the stones and he lost his balance. The glowing end of the iron came down in the very center of my proof sheet which exploded into a thin flash of flame and was gone. The next moment Red and the stranger were rolling on the stones in an untidy heap.

Pierre Gambi and I hurried to help the stranger to his feet again; a difficult task as the man thrashed his long legs about in a peculiarly useless way. On his back he was more like a foolish crane fly than a spider, his legs waving up and down as if of their own accord and his body seeming feeble and silly. When we had got him upright again, Red began to apologize formally for his clumsiness, but the man pushed him aside impatiently.

"Where's the piece of paper I had—very well, boy, stop your gabbling—where's the paper, I say?" he muttered, searching around in the stones at his feet. The paper, of course, was not there. It had gone in smoke and ashes. The stranger gave up the search and turned his suspicious eye on me.

"You're the boy that dropped it, aren't you?"

"Yes, sir," I answered weakly.

"What was it?"

"I don't know," I lied. "I can't read."

He stared at me in silence for a long while and I could see that he did not believe me.

"I shall remember your face," he said at last. "And yours, and yours," he added, turning to the other two. We all kept silent.

"I smell heresy here," the stranger cried, speaking out to the whole company and with some dreadful thing in his voice that made it ring out like the voice of a hunting dog that has scented the stag. "If any of you has information for me, you know where I may be found. God hates heretics and rewards those who help the Church to root them out of our midst." He spread his arms out wide as if to embrace someone. No one stirred or made a sound. Tiny outside noises began to make themselves heard; the sizzling of fat on the roasting eels, a bat squeaking as it hunted over the roof tops, the faint creaking of Red's leather belt as he breathed.

Suddenly the stranger dropped his arms to his sides, turned, and in four swift strides which scattered the pebbles in all directions disappeared into the darkness. The silence was held while you might have counted twenty, then with a sort of sigh those around the fire stirred into life again. Flagons were raised, and a mumble of conversation sprang up.

The eel man said, "You could have chosen a hundred better men to make enemies of. That man never gives up. You may think you're safe because he has turned his back on you, but the day will come when he will spring."

"What can I do?" I said.

"Get as far away from Le Havre as possible—that is, if you have anything to hide—and who hasn't nowadays?"

"But where can I go?" I said to Pierre and Red. "I know no one except Mr. Lebrun in the whole of France. My father is in Geneva. . . ."

"Geneva?" said Red quickly. "You are a Calvinist, then?"

"I suppose so. My father is, at any rate."

"And this Mr. Lebrun?"

"He, too," I said.

"Then you mustn't go back there," said Red. "You might cast suspicion on the house. Somehow we must get you away, and tonight. The question is, how?"

He began to pace up and down in front of us, his shoulders hunched and his thumbs tucked in the front of his belt. Pierre Gambi, who had not spoken for some time, watched him with a knowing smile on his face. Eventually Red sat down again.

"I don't know," he muttered. "If you tried to go across country you would be noticed as a stranger. Unless you know someone who would hide you ... whatever you do, you must take a lot of risks. I'll come with you, if you like, but that might only make things worse. Two are easier to trace than one."

Pierre's smile widened into a grin. "What a fuss and bother you fellows make," he said. "I can get our friend away easily enough."

"Why didn't you say so before?" I asked.

"You might not like my way," said Pierre. "It isn't everybody's meat."

"What is it then?"

"I can't tell you here," he said. "Let's get away to somewhere quieter."

We stood up to go, saying good night to the company.

"I must get word to Mr. Lebrun," I said. "Would he take a message for me?"

Pierre glanced at the eel man and then shook his head. "The daughter would be better," he said. "I'll ask her."

He went over to the girl and had a few muttered words

with her by the eel tank, then he came skipping back to us. "She'll tell them," he said. "Now come with me and we'll find a quiet place to talk. Good night, all!"

Friendly voices answered from around the fire as we followed Pierre out into the darkness.

5

"Well, Pierre?" said Red.

"Well, Pierre?" said Pierre.

"Well, Pierre?" I echoed.

We all laughed, rocking the boat and hearing our laughter bounce back off the harbor walls.

"It's well met," said Red. "The three Pierres, eh?"

"Like bread, butter and cheese," said Pierre Gambi.

"Which is which?" I asked.

"You are the bread," he retorted; "pale, crumbling and a bit soft in the middle."

"But nourishing and dependable," added Red.

"I am the butter," went on Pierre; "rich, slippery and always on top of the bread. And our friend here is the cheese; strong cheese that bites the mouth and is a food all by itself."

We were sitting together in a small boat in the middle of the harbor. The town was dark behind us, and in front the rigging of two ships looked like autumn's skeleton leaves across the sky. The riding lights hanging from mainmast and bowsprit were the only stars.

"Now for your scheme," said Red. "This is a quiet enough place for any number of secrets."

"There's the answer," said Pierre, pointing at the two ships riding at anchor.

"The ships?" I said, excited. "Stow away, you mean?"

"No need to stow away. They'll be glad enough to sign you on."

"Where are they bound for?" asked Red.

"The Americas, of course. You are a couple of country bumpkins, and no mistake."

"The Americas," I said softly. I had heard a little of the new lands to the west, and the word alone was enough to set my mind making strange pictures. "I should be safe there, shouldn't I?"

Pierre laughed. "That's a matter of opinion. You'd be safe enough from old Long Legs. That's one place he'll never follow you to. On the other hand, it's a long voyage and you might go down in a storm or die of scurvy on the way. And even if you got there I don't suppose it would be all roses. The last lot that went did not do so well."

"Why do they go, then, if it's so dangerous?"

"Calvinists, like you," said Pierre shortly. "They got permission to set up a colony in Florida. But most of them prefer to stay at home and take the risk of the Inquisition's getting at them to sailing all that way and then being killed by the Spaniards or the Indians or a fever or starvation or—"

Red laughed. "It can't be all that bad," he said.

"But what will they do when they get there?" I asked. "Will they never come back?"

"They don't mean to," said Pierre. "But why not go on board and see for yourself. They can't eat you."

We agreed and Pierre rowed quickly out to the nearer of the two ships. The deck was in darkness and at first it seemed quite deserted. As we came round her and level

GATHERING THE PEBBLES

with the middle part where the side of the ship was only a few feet above the water, we saw the light of an open fire in a sort of alcove at the foot of the mainmast. A large cauldron of brass was hung over the flames and a little, thin, nervous-looking man was crouched close up to the fire cleaning his fingernails with the point of an immense knife.

"Ahoy, there!" called Pierre softly.

The man looked up from his nails and peered out into the darkness at us. "Ahoy, yourself," he said. "What do you want?"

"May we come aboard?" asked Pierre.

"Do what you like," said the man. "I'm only the cook. It's no business of mine what you do. And the watch is asleep, so he won't stop you."

He went on muttering to himself in a complaining undertone all the time we were tying the boat up and climbing aboard. But immediately we were all on the deck he got to his feet and began to plunge a huge ladle up and down in the cauldron.

"Hungry, I suppose?" he said. "They all are. No bowls with you? Well, you can use mine this time, but you'll have to get fitted up with one each in the morning. Charge you three francs they do, but you can get them in the town for two and a half."

Giving us no chance to reply he thrust three large wooden bowls at us and began to ladle soup out of the cauldron, chattering the whole time.

"Not like I used to make for the bishop. He was a fussy one about his soup. Tip it on the floor he would if it didn't just suit him. He liked to see the grease winking at him as it floated on the top. This will do you, though, if you're hungry. You can't expect anyone to make a real soup with the hind leg of a horse and two laurel leaves. Come on, sup up! There's no horse in this. I was only having my little joke."

We drank the soup down, grinning at one another over the rims of our bowls and saying nothing.

"Well," continued the cook, taking a sip of the soup himself and pursing his lips up critically, "that's how it is. Can't promise it'll always be as good as that. Not enough food aboard by a long shot in my opinion. But, of course, nobody wants my opinion—I'm only the cook. They won't be so high and mighty one of these days when they start feeling hungry and the cook's got nothing for them. Look very nice they do in their gold and silver and soft velvet cloaks, but the belly gets empty just the same no matter how you wrap it in fine linen. A hungry man in brocade and lace is no more than a whited sepulcher, that's what I always say."

At this point the cook suddenly stopped like a mechanism that has gone wrong and sat down behind the fire again.

"Look," said Red bluntly, "we want to find out something about this voyage to the Americas. Can you tell us anything about it?"

The cook went back to cleaning his nails and did not reply.

"But you are sailing to the Americas, aren't you?" I asked.

"How should I know," the man said. "I'm just the cook. Soup and stew, bread and mutton, that's me. I haven't even got a name: I'm just the cook."

"But you know," said Red.

"I'll tell you this," said the cook. "We're sailing sooner or later, and that's certain. Laudonniere's the man in charge and he's been to Florida before so he must know the way. If you want to sign on you'd better see him—or as he's a bit high and mighty perhaps you'd better see the one that's under him. Ottigny, they call him. Nice chap. Flies off the handle if everything's not just right, but a nice chap for all that. He'll fix you up."

"Where can we find him?" asked Pierre.

"He's ashore," said the cook. "They're all ashore. They've gone to a meeting in the square. Why they can't meet on the ship beats me. Just looking for trouble, that's what they are. I said as much to them, but who listens to the cook? Off they went, all the gentlemen pulling their swords round to a handy place and loosening them in the scabbards and smiling and laughing. There'll be trouble before the morning, I said. But nobody paid any attention."

"Well," said Red, "what shall we do? Wait here until they come back, or go and look for them?"

"We might miss them," I said. "Let's stay here."

"Let's go ashore," said Pierre. "There might be some fun."

Red considered for a moment. "Yes," he said, "let's go ashore. You can stay here if you want to—"

"No," I said quickly. "I'll come with you."

6

Ten minutes later we were back in the town making for the square where the cook had said he thought the meeting was to be held. The other two were talking excitedly of what might happen, and Pierre Gambi especially was skipping about as if he were going to a party. I did not feel so pleased with the idea myself. I gathered that just at the moment the Huguenots were in rather a strange position. By the law of France they were criminals, but for some reason or other the state was leaving them alone. They were even permitted to hold meetings in public places and spread their religion, but at the very same time the Church might be arresting individual Huguenots and trying them for heresy.

Certain groups of people of the old Church had decided to take the law into their own hands. They had formed little bands of armed fanatics, and these bands wandered about seeking out Huguenot meetings and attacking them. The Huguenots, being mostly merchants or traders or business folk, did not usually carry arms, but the few young noblemen who had joined them formed themselves into defence groups. Whenever there was a Huguenot meeting these young noblemen would form a ring round the outside of the crowd and protect them from attack. I did not like the sound of it at all.

The streets we passed through were all deserted, and for a while I hoped that the journey would come to nothing and that eventually we should sensibly go back to the ship and wait. But then we reached the square and found it crowded, and my hopes vanished. Five or six hundred people were massed together in the center around the foot of the monument there, and a man standing up on the plinth was talking to them in an excited way. I don't know what he was saying, for we were too far away to hear and could not get into the crowd.

What worried me was the ring of armed gentlemen around the crowd. They were standing five or six paces from each other and turned outwards with their backs to the speaker at the center. They seemed to be watching the streets which led into the square, and some of them were fidgeting with the handles of their swords, drawing them out of the scabbard an inch or so and then letting them drop back. They would not let us through, so in the end we stood back at the side of the square under an overhanging shop front and waited for the meeting to finish.

The man on the plinth ended and got down, and another man took his place. He wore the brown habit of a wandering friar and his head was shaven except for a narrow ring of gray hair. I knew that many of the wandering friars had accepted the new faith, and were looked on in some quarters as troublemakers, so I feared the worst.

Again, it was impossible to hear what he was saying, but from the way he swung his arms about and sweated in the torchlight I guessed he was working the crowd up. They all began to get restless, crying and groaning as the friar spoke. There was a sort of restless movement, too, as when an uncertain wind blows over a June meadow when the grasses are seeding.

Then suddenly there came a loud shout of "On guard!" from one of the gentlemen, and then the long sickening sound of steel sliding as swords everywhere were drawn. The friar stopped speaking and the heads in the crowd turned this way and that trying to seek out the direction of the disturbance. Like sheep when driven by a new and unknown dog the people huddled together, those on the outside trying to get nearer to the center and away from the danger.

For a moment no one could see where the attack was coming from, then twenty or thirty young men came running out of the street on our left and checked within a dozen paces of the crowd. A sort of moan of dismay came up from the people, and then there was absolute silence as the two parties stood facing each other. The armed men of each party now had their swords out and most of them crouched forward slightly, sword point just touching the ground in front, waiting.

"Down with all heretics!" shouted one of the attackers.

The crowd howled aloud with one voice.

One of the youngest of the attackers, he could not have been more than sixteen or seventeen, bent and picked a stray cobble from the road and hurled it into the center of the crowd, screaming something, and then waved his sword and rushed forward to the attack. The group followed him, shouting too, and immediately the square was a turmoil of struggling, shouting people. Some of the crowd on the far side of the square broke out and ran down one of the side streets, but the majority stayed where they were, just pressing closer together and waiting to see what would happen.

The gang that was attacking the crowd was easily outnumbered by the defenders, but because of the speed of their attack and the fact that half the defending party were on the far side of the crowd and took some time to get round, the attackers for the moment had the advantage. The actual fighting was only between the armed parties but the impetus of the attack carried it well into the edges of the crowd. Women were screaming with fear and trying to drag their children out of the way. People were falling and being trampled on, and as many of the torches were put out in the scuffle, it was hard to tell exactly what was happening.

I was quite paralyzed by the whole scene, standing back against the shop and staring horrified at all that went on. It was as if I had been looking at some painting of an angry crowd which had suddenly come to life, and all the horror of it, which before had been hidden under the coldness of old paint had now burst over me in a great gush.

The other two were not affected in the same way. Pierre drew the short poignard he wore at his belt and rushed into the crowd shouting something over his shoulder as he went. Red was pulling at the shutter of the shop front, trying to tear off a plank for a cudgel and shouting again and again, "We must do something! Great heavens, we must do something!"

At that moment a pair of men, fencing skilfully as if they were alone, completely oblivious of the crowd on all sides, backing in our direction. One of them, from the Huguenot meeting, I had noticed already. He was dressed almost entirely in crimson satin which shone like polished steel in the torchlight. He wore an absurd felt hat with a long yellow feather, and his hair, which he wore very long, fell on his shoulders. He was clearly a foreigner. He was shouting gaily and laughing as he fought, whereas his opponent, a short swarthy man, was fighting grimly and with venom, his lips compressed in a straight line.

"Well done!" cried the foreigner when his opponent's sword passed through his satin sleeve. "That's two I owe you. Arlac always pays his debts."

They came to a stand just in front of us, their swords flickering and crossing and giving off harsh screams as edge ran on edge.

"Ah, you tire, it seems," muttered the gay foreigner, and he pressed forward against his enemy, thrusting and parrying even more quickly than before. A look of fear came over the face of the swarthy man as if he knew that he was outmatched and that the end was only a few moments away.

But before that moment arrived, a woman with a baby in her arms came blindly out of the crowd and collided with the brightly dressed foreigner, throwing him off his balance. His sword flew into the air and stuck point first into one of the old wooden beams of the overhanging story above us. The other man drew back his sword for the final thrust and as he did so his eyes flickered over the foreigner's body as of choosing the best place to strike. The foreigner was on one knee, his face turned up with an expression half-grin, half-snarl, with white teeth bared.

I shut my eyes and then opened them again immediately as a loud choking cry came from one of the two men. But instead of the foreigner transfixed by the sword, I saw the other man lying on the cobbles with a long oaken post across his chest. The foreigner, this Arlac, jumped to his feet and ran at Red with his arms outstretched. Red started to laugh and then disappeared into the foreigner's hug.

"It was just a lucky blow," he said, emerging at last.

"Lucky?" said Arlac, embracing him again. "It was perfect. Ah, my friend, you saw it?" He turned to me and I shook my head. "Whoooup!" he said. "Right in the ear. Magnificent. I am very grateful."

"I couldn't get the thing loose," said Red. "It was the shutter bar, you see. And then when it came there was this chap just going for you. So I let him have it."

Arlac bent over the unconscious man and pulled off his belt and scabbard. Then he picked up the sword and handed them both to Red. "There you are," he said. "You have earned them. Come on! We waste time."

He pulled his own sword out of the wooden beam and turned with Red towards the crowd.

But by now the fight was over. The attack had been beaten off and the wounded were already being attended to.

"It is finished," Arlac exclaimed. "We are too late."

Pierre returned just then, grinning and shaking his head. "That was a bit of fun," he said. "I wouldn't have missed that. These Huguenots are tough chaps. There was a big fishmonger there, did you see him? He pulled off his boot and walloped them over the head with it. He got five of them all by himself. What a lad!"

The three of them talked about the fighting for a while and then Arlac said, "Well, I must get back to the ship. I see the crowd is dispersing now."

"Are you from the ship in the harbor, then?" asked Red. "The one bound for Florida?"

"Yes, indeed," said Arlac. "You too?"

"Well, no," said Red. "But my friend here wants a passage, and we were trying to find out something about it."

"Your friend?" Arlac looked at me as if seeing me for the first time and did not seem to be much interested in what he saw. "But I could arrange that for you. Have you not saved my life? For you I would arrange anything. But why don't you come too? It will be good fun, this. An adventure, eh? New lands, new people, new everything. You should come."

Red hesitated only a moment. "Why not?" he said.

Arlac caught him round the waist and swung him in a sort of wild dance. "That will be wonderful," he cried. "Come back with me now and I shall fix it all up."

There was nothing to keep us. The square was almost deserted now. I had no home to go back to, and only adventure in front. We began to say good-by to Pierre Gambi and thank him for all he had done.

"It was nothing," he said. "Nothing at all. I wouldn't have missed parts of it for a hundred francs," and he winked at me as he said the last part, from which I understood that the little affair in the harbor was to be forgotten.

"Why don't you come also?" asked Arlac.

"I'm not a Huguenot," said Pierre. "I'm not anything, really."

"What does that matter?" said Arlac. "Adventure is for everyone. Say you will come!"

"It might be a bit of fun," said Pierre thoughtfully. "Do these Indian fellows have any money?"

"They eat off solid gold plates," laughed Arlac, "and the little children play marbles with diamonds and rubies and pearls."

"That's the place for me," exclaimed Pierre. "Sign me on, too!"

7

So the three Pierres embarked on the *Elizabeth of Honfluer* for the Americas. We did not sail immediately, for there was a third ship which came up from La Rochelle to join us, but on the 20th May, 1564, the little fleet, under the command of Réné de Laudonniere, with four hundred and twenty-seven colonists crowded into every nook and cranny of the vessels, drew out of the harbor at Le Havre and stood out to sea. The adventure had begun.

Chapter Two

THE INDIANS

WE SIGHTED the coast of Florida on Thursday the 22nd July, quite early in the morning. It was low, flat country, scarcely above sea level, so that we were almost up to it before the lookout sang out that there was land ahead. By the middle of the afternoon the three ships were in the mouth of a river which made a good natural harbor.

Laudonniere had been ill for the previous week and had not shown his face on deck. He lay in his bunk staring and staring at the ceiling, slowly twisting his long white fingers in his beard, sweating, feverish and silent. All the business of the voyage was done through Ottigny, who was the only person other than myself allowed into the cabin. And I was not exactly allowed in, but sent in, much against my will, to serve Laudonniere with food and drink, and for the rest of the time to sit quietly in a corner in case he needed something. I did this very unwillingly.

I was frightened by the gaunt, silent man who seldom moved and who seemed to be sinking into a sort of trance. To tell the truth, I thought he was dying of fever and that I should certainly catch it through sitting near him. The cabin was heavy with the smell of sickness and as the surgeon would not allow the porthole to be opened but had it and the door sealed up with strips of felt the atmosphere was so heavy that it was often a labor to breathe. I must admit that whenever I slipped out to get food for Laudonniere I stayed on deck much longer than was necessary, breathing deep and yawning and stretching my arms as if I had just been released from an airless dungeon.

On the Thursday morning that land was sighted, Ottigny came in with the good news.

"We have sighted land, sir," he reported. "Vasseur, the navigator, says we are too far south, but he wants the fleet to anchor near the shore so that he can make a more accurate calculation."

Laudonniere continued to stare at the ceiling as if he had not heard. Ottigny glanced over at me in my corner and gave me a friendly smile and then looked back at Laudonniere, waiting for instructions. After a long silence Laudonniere groaned and turned his face to the wall.

"We have sighted land, sir," Ottigny repeated, bending forward a little and frowning in a worried sort of way.

"I heard you, curse you, I heard," shouted Laudonniere in a high, cracked voice. "We've sighted land but the navigator does not know whether it is Florida or the Azores. Everything always miscarries." The last three words he said in a low shaking voice, and when he turned his face for an instant I could see that his eyes had tears in them.

"No, sir," said Ottigny gently. "It is not so serious. We are a little south of our objective, but on the same coast."

"Everything always miscarries," repeated Laudonniere faintly.

"There is no need to anchor if you do not wish it," said Ottigny. "We simply need to coast northward until we strike the River of May. Would you rather we did that?"

"I would rather you left me in peace," said Laudonniere. "Leave me alone. Decide what you will, but leave me alone." He pulled the covers completely over his head.

Ottigny stood for a moment not sure what to do, then he shrugged his shoulders and left. There was complete silence in the cabin for a very long time after this. After a while I thought that Laudonniere was asleep and I went to creep quietly from the cabin.

"Where are you going, boy?" he asked softly, rolling over to look at me when my hand rattled the door latch.

"Nowhere, sir," I said. "At least, I thought you were asleep and I was going..." I was confused and a little frightened of his eyes which seemed for a moment to be holes reaching through his head down deep into the earth itself.

"You wanted to get out of this prison for a few minutes," he said.

"No, sir. It's only that the air is a little close."

"Come over here," he said. "Nearer!" I went up to the

bunk. "Now put your hand on my forehead!" I did so, fearing still. His skin was cold and damp like an old rock that lies near a waterfall.

"That is the prison," he said quietly. "Only my head. We are not in a prison; the prison is in us. You can go out on the deck in a moment and breathe the air which to you seems fresh and new and full of adventure. I cannot go anywhere and leave my head behind, and to me even the air that seeps in through the closed porthole reeks of death and misery and ... and vile things that you know nothing about."

"I'm sorry, sir," I said. I could not think of anything else to say, and in any case I *was* sorry for him.

"Are you?" he said. Then he sat up and stared closely at me. "Are you?" he repeated. "Maybe you can help me. Boys enjoy stories, don't they? Will you listen while I tell you a story?"

"Yes, sir," I said.

"Sit down, then. Here, close to me."

The heat of the cabin swept over me for a moment and I thought I should faint. Nevertheless I went to sit on the side of his bunk as he had ordered, only glancing for a second at the blue sky through the porthole. Maybe it was that brief glance that made him change his mind.

"Not now," he muttered suddenly. "Some other time."

He lay back on the bunk and began to run his fingers fretfully through his beard again.

"I should like to help," I said nervously.

"Thank you," he said dully. "But go now. Go up on the deck and see the new land. Look at the trees and the sand and the colored birds. Fill your eyes with it all for the first time, and remember it well."

"Will you be all right, sir?" I said, my legs already carrying me towards the door and the open air.

"I shall sleep," he said.

But as I closed the door behind me, I saw that his eyes were still open and that he stared at the ceiling. I stole away on deck with a guilty feeling of having somehow betrayed him.

2

We anchored in the river mouth barely a hundred yards from the southern bank and the captain sent two boats ashore with empty water casks. We had no immediate need of fresh water but he was a fussy man and did not like to see his boats going off without achieving something useful.

Arlac took one of the boats and a man called François de la Caille the other. La Caille was a sergeant and was in charge of the troops. He was a nobleman and an important person in the expedition, coming next in authority to Ottigny. He had been with Laudonniere on the first voyage to Florida and from the way he refused to talk about his experiences, it was generally assumed either that he had made a great fortune from the voyage, or that things had happened which were best not talked about. He was a tall man, very stiff in his way of walking. He seemed only able to bend at one place—his hips—so that when he sat down, which he did very seldom, he looked rather like a carved wooden doll. He had long curved moustaches, like bull's horns only more drooping, and a bright red face that shone constantly with perspiration. He was a kindly man and we liked him.

La Caille took Red in his boat to carry the cask and Arlac took me. As the boats headed for the beach there was a great deal of laughter and gay chatter, and the crews pulled hard.

"Who'll be the first ashore?" cried Arlac. "Keep the time, now. One, two, one, two, pull, back, pull, back..." He jumped up in the stern and bent over the crew shouting the time and urging them on. The other boat had the lead to start with, but when we drew level they too heaved harder on their oars and La Caille swayed backwards and forwards booming at them.

The two boats shot forward with a great rustling of water and creaking of wood. The men pulled as if they were being flogged, their eyes glazed and empty and their mouths hanging open as they gulped in the air.

"Pull, back, pull, back," shouted Arlac, his voice going higher and higher in his excitement.

"Boom, boom, boom," went La Caille's voice.

Our boat was a bare half-length ahead when it grounded on the sand. We scrambled over the thwarts and fell into the warm water laughing and struggling with one another and went towards the beach on all fours, because there did not seem time to stand up. And after all that it was Red who was first ashore. He jumped clean off the stern of his boat on to dry sand. I saw him go flying over my head while I was still floundering in the shallow water.

The crews lay flat on the warm sand, panting and exhausted, but the rest of us went to the top of the beach and into the shade of the trees. The river must have flooded fairly regularly for we could not go straight into the forest until we had climbed over a jumble of whitened wood and plant stems, bones and forest rubbish, that lay heaped at the flood line. It was a good ten feet high and it struck me that the inhabitants could not want for firewood, which was a silly thought since the forest in front might well, for all I knew, go on for a thousand miles with enough wood in it to keep all the fires in creation going forever.

La Caille picked up a string of leather beads among the driftwood and we left him prodding about there, muttering, and went into the trees. Bright birds, which except for some like parrots were all new to me, flew away from us through the trees, squawking and screaming, and something furry and brown ran quickly among the trunks and disappeared.

"Fresh meat for supper," cried Arlac and ran ahead with his arquebus. Red and I, struggling with the water casks, were left behind.

As we went deeper into the forest I began to feel strangely uncomfortable. The land was low and damp and heavy with smells of rotting vegetation, and the sun shining between the trees only served to raise a thin steam from the waterlogged ground. I was afraid of snakes and things that crawl, and even more afraid of things I did not know about. Many of the trees had long beards and whispers of pale green moss so that they looked like old old men who had been cast ashore and forgotten.

"We shan't find any fresh water in a place like this," I said. "It's almost a marsh here."

"I suppose you're right," said Red. "Anyway, the place gives me the shivers. Just look at that snake!"

He pointed up at a tall tree festooned with some sort of flowering creeper, and I saw an immense snake with brightly patterned skin hanging in a loop from one of the boughs. Its head was hanging down with bright eyes looking at us, and as we hurried past the head turned slowly and resentfully as if its owner would have liked to come a little closer and within range.

"I expect it's harmless enough," said Red.

"I don't expect anything of the sort," I said. "I wonder where Arlac's got to?"

As if in answer there came the sharp flat crack of the arquebus going off, followed immediately by a shout of triumph. It did not sound very far off so we waited a few minutes, and soon Arlac broke through the undergrowth and came towards us. He was carrying a small creature over his shoulder, scarcely larger than a greyhound and something of the same build. It had delicately curved horns and its coat was mottled fawn and brown. I should think it was some sort of small deer.

But before we could admire the creature, or Arlac's skill in killing it, the sound of a horn from the ship reached us. It was the signal for the return of the boats and we made for the beach as quickly as possible.

"Now what's happened?" muttered Arlac.

I had a faint idea, but said nothing, only hurried with the others for the boat. The crews were at their oars already, and La Caille was just getting aboard when we came out of the trees.

"Wait for us!" shouted Red.

La Caille looked up and waved violently. "Hurry!" he shouted. "They've got their anchor up. Something must be wrong."

"What can be wrong?" panted Arlac. He had a job to keep up with us, burdened with the deer and his heavy arquebus. And it was hard to see what could have gone wrong. The sky was absolutely cloudless and the sea empty and calm as far as one could see. Both banks of the river were deserted, and no movement other than our own disturbed the place. However, we hurried.

Immediately we were in the boats the rowers pulled away and in a very short time we were up with the ships which had already begun to turn and hoist sail. We clambered on board feeling a little irritated at our outing's being spoilt.

"What's up?" shouted Arlac. "What's gone wrong?"

"You may well ask," answered Ottigny who was standing near. "Who fired that shot?"

"I did, of course," said Arlac. "Look what I got with it."

"You're wanted below," said Ottigny tersely.

Arlac dropped his burden on the deck with a clatter and put both hands on his hips. "Well," he exploded, "it's come to something if I'm to be treated like a naughty schoolboy."

But before he could get any further the cabin door on the lower deck opened and Laudonniere came slowly out into the sunlight.

"Look at all those dolphins!" shouted a harsh voice from the side: it was Jacques le Moyne, the artist, whose official job was map making. "Just look at them!"

Laudonniere paused a moment and looked over the side to where a dozen or more dolphins were leaping almost alongside the ship, then he put both hands to his face for a second and turned back towards his cabin as if he had forgotten why he had come out.

Ottigny called out, "The two boats are back, sir."

Laudonniere hesitated and then started to climb the

short companionway towards where we were all standing. Everybody stood perfectly still, waiting while he came up.

"Yes," said Laudonniere. He stood in front of us letting his glance run slowly from La Caille to Arlac, from Arlac to Ottigny and then back to La Caille. He seemed to be in some sort of trance, his finely cut features swollen slightly and his eyelids down, half-covering his eyes. Finally he noticed the animal lying on the deck at Arlac's feet and the arquebus beside it. He stared at Arlac.

"You fired a shot," he said, not asking a question.

"I did," said Arlac standing very straight and going a bright pink. Laudonniere leaned forward and with his open hand gave the Swiss a heavy blow across the face. There was absolute silence, absolute stillness over the whole of the ship. Arlac did not move to retaliate. His face showed only a mixture of perhaps surprise and pity.

"Fool, fool, fool!" said Laudonniere in a hoarse voice. "That one shot might be enough to bring the Spaniards about our ears. You know as well as I do that all this is Spanish soil and that we are far from welcome here. It is bad enough that an incompetent navigator should bring us too far south; to shout our presence across the forest is sheer lunacy."

"I am not afraid of the Spaniards, sir," said Arlac. "They are only men."

"It is easy for a fool to be brave," sneered Laudonniere. "If you were responsible for four hundred lives as I am you would be afraid. You have a position of authority and yet you behave like a schoolboy. My responsibilities are great enough as it is without people like you adding to the burden. Is this the beast you shot?"

Arlac nodded.

Laudonniere bent suddenly and stroked the soft pale ears of the dead deer. "These cannot be tamed," he said. "I have tried, but they pine and die in captivity." Then as suddenly his mood changed and he rose to his feet and said harshly, "Throw the beast overboard!"

There was a faint murmur of protest from one or two standing around who were looking on the first fresh meat for a month. Arlac, however, picked up the deer without a word and hurled it over the side into the sea. Laudonniere returned to his cabin, moving clumsily like a man half blind.

As the cabin door closed La Caille said explosively, "My God, he would not have struck me so! I should not have borne it. Why, man, are you made of milk?"

"He was right and I was wrong," said Arlac simply. And then he added with a self-conscious grin. "And besides, I *am* afraid of the Spaniards."

"I don't believe it," said La Caille. "That man is ill to madness, behaving in such a way before everyone. He destroys everyone else's authority, and is himself unfit to hold a command. How can we keep our oath of allegiance to him when—"

Arlac gripped La Caille quickly by the arm and stopped him. "There will be plenty of mutiny and evil behavior before this expedition is over," he said quietly. "I should be unhappy to think anyone here a party to it. A sick leader needs healthy lieutenants."

La Caille did not speak for a moment, then he turned and gripped the Swiss firmly by both arms. "Friend Arlac," he said, "I thank you for two valuable lessons.

First, on the true meaning of loyalty, and second, on how a man may show his bravery by acting the coward."

3

For the next three days we coasted northwards, watching the dark green forests slip by. Laudonniere did not appear on deck but I continued to serve him in his cabin. His health seemed to improve and he spent most of the time going through the records of stores and equipment.

The third day was a Sunday and he was making ready to attend the service that would be held as usual on deck when Ottigny came in with news.

He said, "The navigator is certain we have reached the River of May. Will you come and identify it, sir?"

Laudonniere nodded and went out with him and I followed. Most of the crew were on deck waiting for the service, staring meanwhile at the coast. We had just come level with a wide opening in the land that might have been the mouth of a river. The trees presented the same unchanging green wall that they had done for the last three days, but at one point five or six miles inland there seemed to be a slight rise in the level of the forest which formed a sort of knoll or bluff.

Laudonniere gave the scene the merest of glances. "The River of May," he said. "We will anchor off the south bank. The bottom is good there. I shall stand by the helmsman myself and direct him."

In a short time the ship heeled over on its new course, and the other two ships, observing us, followed in towards the river mouth. Laudonniere had suddenly become a new man. He gave orders in a crisp, certain voice, and moved about the decks with a sort of restrained eagerness. He gave orders that two of the boats were to go ashore immediately the anchoring had been completed. He and Le Moyne were to take one, Ottigny and La Caille the other. Four soldiers to each boat were to be armed, two with arquebus and two with crossbow. "A Pierre to each boat for ballast," he added with something approaching a smile, and then under his breath, "and for good luck." Pierre Gambi and myself were chosen and I went with Laudonniere's boat.

We went off cautiously towards the shore, not racing this time but approaching the empty beach slowly, scanning the forest. The soldiers held their guns and bows at the ready, four of them blowing gently on their matches to keep the glow bright in case they had to fire at short notice.

I was sitting next to Le Moyne, the artist, and was amused to see how nervous he was getting. He kept thrusting his hands between his knees and gripping them tight, but after a moment they would stray out and his broad, coarse fingers would begin to tap on the wooden thwart. His square, ugly face, pock-marked and lopsided, was almost white, and his eyes looked out from under his heavy, straw-colored eyebrows with suspicion and a touch of fear.

He was a simple fellow, Le Moyne, with a sort of innocent, credulous attitude to everything. This made him often the subject of rough jokes, but he took them very well. In many ways he was like a child, but his drawings, which he made very quickly and without any obvious care, were always exact and full of detail. Sometimes he would glance at something as if he only half saw it and had no interest in it whatever. But when he came to make his drawing, you saw that he had been noticing even the tiniest of things. The only man on board he seemed to have any time for was La Caille. They did not talk much together but were, as Le Moyne himself put it, "fond of each other's silence."

While I had been thinking about Le Moyne, the boats had reached the shore, but no one landed. Laudonniere was standing up searching the length of the beach and in no hurry to go farther. One of the crew said softly, "Quiet as a grave! I bet there's not an Indian for a hundred miles."

"More likely an Indian behind every tree," said Laudonniere quickly. "I know these people. I landed at this very spot two years ago. Yes, and embarked from it not long after. There was no lack of Indians then."

But still nothing stirred on the beach, and the colored birds flitted about in the trees as if they had the forest all to themselves. At last Laudonniere motioned the armed men to land first and spread along the beach ten or twelve yards apart to cover our landing. They did this with caution, infected perhaps by his example, pointing their weapons into the woods and now and then glancing nervously over their shoulders to make sure we were not deserting them.

Laudonniere then stepped ashore and raising his head shouted aloud the one word, "Saturiba!"

Before the echo had died away a small party of Indians suddenly appeared in front of the trees. It was like magic; first there had been no one, and now there were fifteen or twenty strangely clad figures standing watching us. A man, who was obviously the leader, stood out in front of them and shouted something. He was the tallest of the Indians, though not unusually tall. He was almost naked except for a sort of leather skirt decorated with dabs of clay and little hanging tufts of dark red moss. His hair had clay in it, stuck with bright feathers. The clay had hardened and whitened in the sun so that his long black hair stood some way out from his head with the ends trailing out behind like a plume. He wore a quiver of arrows at his back but carried no bow, and as he advanced he spread both hands out, palms uppermost, as if to show that he was unarmed.

Laudonniere frowned for a moment, muttering, "That is not Saturiba. He was a heavier man altogether and ..." Nevertheless he held his hands up in an imitation of the Indian's gesture and took a few steps in front of our little group, calling out a dozen words or so in a strange language.

The Indian chief and Laudonniere advanced slowly towards each other, meeting in the clear open space between us. They embraced, giving each other great bearlike hugs and began to speak in the Indian's language.

After a few minutes Laudonniere turned and called to us. "This is the native chief of all these parts," he said. "Bow to him as you would to an earl or a count. He is a simple fellow and it will please him. Besides, we shall be depending on him and his tribe for food until we have settled in."

We all bowed solemnly and the Indian seemed delighted. Pierre Gambi played the fool by performing an elaborate court bow and then kissing the chief's hand as if he were royalty itself. Laudonniere frowned a little but did not say anything.

Then the chief called up his followers and led forward two youngsters, very powerfully built and about fifteen or sixteen years old. They were his sons, it seemed. One of them came over to me and stared into my eyes for a long while without speaking. Then he produced a wedge of solid silver from under his skirt—it was rather like a piece of cheese in shape—and put it in my hand. I smiled and thanked him, although of course he could not understand my words.

"You must give something in return," said Laudonniere. "It is the native custom. And if he doesn't like what you give him he will take his gift back."

I dug into my pockets and fetched out a variety of objects, and the Indian immediately seized on a crumbled scrap of paper on which I had scribbled a message which I had delivered for Laudonniere a few days before. He smoothed it out and studied the writing intently as if trying to read it, then put it carefully in his mouth and ate it.

"Whatever is he up to?" I asked.

Laudonniere shrugged his shoulders. "I expect he thinks the writing was white man's magic, so he has eaten it to get some of the magic inside him."

In any case the Indian seemed very pleased with himself and strutted about among the others pointing to his mouth and then tapping himself on the chest as if to show what a great fellow he was.

Meanwhile the chief had taken Laudonniere aside and with the tip of one of his arrows was making a series of rough scratches in the sand. He kept pointing away behind him, apparently into the woods, and then running the arrow tip again over some of the lines already marked. Laudonniere was puzzled and could not understand the Indian's meaning. Pierre Gambi, however, quicker witted than the rest of us perhaps, suddenly exclaimed:

"It's a sort of map. Look, he means this to be the river. It must be the water of two or three streams, and there are islands, see? And it rises somewhere in the south."

"Of course," agreed Laudonniere. "I have been up the river a short way. It is like that."

The chief saw that we understood his meaning and went on with his map. All around the area he marked a boundary line and then indicating the part enclosed he pointed inland over the tops of the trees. "Saturiba!" he said, and then bowed down towards the direction his finger pointed.

"He means Saturiba rules over all that area," said La Caille, and then asked the chief a short question. "Yes, that's right," he added to us. "This is Saturiba's country and this fellow is one of the lesser tribal chiefs under him."

The Indian then pointed his arrow tip a long way south on the map, not far from the source of the river and well outside Saturiba's frontier. He drew in the sand a group of rounded huts and beside them a man with a club.

"Outina!"

"Another Indian tribe," I suggested.

"Another king, perhaps," said Laudonniere. "The tribes group together into confederacies for protection, and sooner or later one of the chiefs dominates the others."

The chief then drew another group of Indian huts and

another man with a club, to the west this time and far inland. "Potanou!" he said. Obviously three rival kings. We showed that we understood.

"I wonder how important these other chiefs are?" said Ottigny.

But the Indian had not finished. He now rose to his feet and began to make a circuit of the map. He walked with bent back and exaggerated high steps as if he were pretending to creep. It seemed to be some sort of dance. When he reached the drawing of the chief called Outina he suddenly sprang back as if he had been burned and went through an elaborate shadow fight, ducking and weaving and striking at his imaginary enemy with an imaginary club. At the same time his followers on the beach began to howl and shout in a sort of ecstasy. The fight ended with—apparently—a victory for our Indian and he then continued his prowl until he reached the drawing of Potanou. The Indians howled again and the chief fought again. This time the two sons joined in the battle and the victory was even more thorough. The demonstration was over.

"Well done," said Laudonniere and clapped the chief on the back. "Well fought!"

La Caille however shook his head doubtfully. "I take that to mean," he mumbled, "that the great chief Saturiba is not friends with his neighbors. Which is his business, of course. But it will be a bad day for us if we get entangled in Indian warfare. If the tribes are running a three-cornered war here it will be very difficult to keep ourselves out of it."

"Nonsense!" exclaimed Laudonniere. "Have you not heard of Cortez, the Spaniard, and how he conquered

Mexico? He took the whole country with only a tiny handful of men, simply by supporting one warring tribe against the other and so letting the Indians do his fighting for him. This is our opportunity. When we meet this Saturiba we must offer him our support."

He went forward quickly, and taking the chief by the arm, drew him once more in a circuit of the map. This time, when they came level with Outina and his camp Laudonniere himself made a grimace of rage and drew his sword. The Indian stared at him for a moment, not understanding, and then he grasped the idea. The two of them, French nobleman and Indian savage, went through the pantomime battle side by side.

The other Indians screamed and capered with delight and then ran forward and taking others of us by the hand persuaded us to join in the battle. Soon we were all leaping and shouting like madmen and doing frightful damage to the poor Outina and his unsuspecting tribe. It must have appeared quite ridiculous.

I noticed that La Caille alone did not join in. He shook off the young Indian who was trying to persuade him and went away up the beach by himself, a stiff, angular and disapproving figure.

Later, when we were returning to the boats, Ottigny said, "That was either a piece of brilliant statesmanship or a foolhardy risk. I wonder which?"

"Statesmanship often includes the taking of risks," said Laudonniere buoyantly. "But I take it that you disapprove, Sergeant La Caille? May I have your reasons?"

La Caille opened his mouth to speak and then caught Ottigny's eye and the warning expression on his face. He hesitated, and then said gruffly, "My joints are a little stiff for such exercise, sir. I did not intend to give offense."

Laudonniere let the incident drop, and as we rowed back to the boat, we chatted about the silver I had been given and the pieces of solid gold some of the Indians had been wearing for decoration.

4

The next morning Laudonniere told Ottigny that he would take a party ashore to explore the river a little and find if the place would do for a settlement. He said that he would take only twenty armed men and one of the officers—Vasseur, La Caille, Arlac or Ottigny. I did not care for Vasseur, who was a dried-up sort of man, like a retired grocer, very mean and given to telling exaggerated stories about himself. The officers were to draw lots and all the remainder would stay on board until he returned.

When the news got around there was a great deal of dissatisfaction, especially from the people on one of the other ships. A man called Auguste Fourneaux rowed over to complain about Laudonniere's "highhanded treatment," as he called it, but Laudonniere would not see him. Fourneaux then complained publicly from the deck and caused something of a commotion. He said that it was all very well for the soldiers who were paid by the day whether they lay in their bunks or went ashore, but what about those who had come to found a new colony? He said they had endured a poor voyage and were eager to see the new land. Some of the settlers on board began to agree with him and sent a deputation to Laudonniere to demand that they be allowed to land. But although the deputation stood outside Laudonniere's door for half an hour or so shouting their complaints through the thick wooden planks, it was not opened to them and Laudonniere did not appear.

At last Fourneaux drew them aside and I overheard him say that they would go ashore whether or not they had permission. "Wait until the old fox is safely up the river," he said, "and we will do as we please."

As I was not there to see I am not quite certain whether they did go ashore after that. Nothing was ever said about it, but I rather gathered from their attitude later that they had taken a look at the land and not thought much of it.

At last Fourneaux went back grumbling to his ship and Laudonniere emerged from his cabin. He had dressed himself in flowered silk and trimmed and scented his beard as if to attend a Court function. He seemed in a high good humor, and as he said nothing about the noise there had been on the deck earlier, no one dared to spoil his good temper by bringing that matter up.

Ottigny drew lucky and was with the party, and he picked Red, Pierre Gambi and myself to go with them. Le Moyne went as a matter of course. He seemed to be a free agent and did pretty well what he pleased, as I suppose was only right as he was the official artist and was expected to keep some sort of record of what occurred. As we climbed into the boats he handed to me a great satchel to carry, stuffed with papers and equipment. I should have liked to dump it in the sea, but he kept a very close watch on me all day and I almost put my shoulder out hauling the thing around for him.

The carpenter had stepped a mast in each boat and rigged some small square sails so that we went up the river in fine style with the wind almost behind us. We had scarcely gone half a mile, however, when there was a great noise of shouting on the bank and half a dozen of the local tribesmen came dancing down to the water's edge and put out in an ugly dugout canoe.

They looked very different and warlike, and for a few minutes we feared they were going to attack us. Laudonniere said that these Indians usually fought naked or nearly so and that the highly decorated costumes they wore were reserved for ceremonial occasions. It was not only their costumes that were decorated, either.

These six Indians had shirts or coats of soft pale brown leather on which were sewn patterns made of the quills of the porcupine. The quills had been dyed various colors and were arranged mostly in stars and zigzags. Their faces and legs were decorated, too, with some sort of paint, and their hair was molded into fantastic shapes with white clay. Their ears were slit and in each ear they wore the float of a fish, either silver, as it is by nature, or dyed a deep crimson.

When they came up with us there was a long parley which no one could properly understand. We gathered that they wanted us to land or the chief would be profoundly annoyed. Laudonniere ordered us to turn to the shore.

The Indians let us into the wood to a distance of about a quarter of a mile where the trees fell back to form an almost circular glade. In the center of this space there was a stone column ten or twelve feet high set on a square stone plinth and engraved with lettering.

"That's no Indian work," said Ottigny.

"The column!" exclaimed Laudonniere. "I had quite forgotten it." He stared at the monument with a peculiar expression, as if it had reproached him. When he saw us all looking at him he turned away and tried to speak normally, but I could see that his forehead was suddenly wet with perspiration. "It is a column Jean Ribaut had erected on the first visit made to these parts," he said. "It gives the names of the men who were with him, as you'll see when we come closer to it."

"The Indians seem to have a queer respect for it," said Red.

He was right. About forty or fifty of them were seated round the column in a circle solemnly staring, while at the foot of the plinth the chief himself was on his knees with his head bowed down almost to the ground. Wreaths of bright flowers were hung about the stone, and large flat woven baskets full of cooked food stood before it. It looked as if some sort of heathen worship were in progress.

As we approached, the chief got up and greeted us and embarked on a long speech during which he indicated first us and then the column as if we were in some way associated. Pierre Gambi nudged me while this was going on.

"It strikes me," he whispered, "that we're desperately short of interpreters in these parts. Laudonniere knows a few words and that La Caille a bit more, but to the rest of us it's all Greek. Anyone who could speak these savages' jabber would be in a very comfortable position."

"How do you mean?"

"Why," he answered, "the whole expedition would depend on him, that's what I mean. You could name your own price, see? Just think of it!"

I didn't think of it, but he obviously did, as he later proved; but more of that when the time comes.

Meanwhile the chief had finished his speech and persuaded us all to sit down, whereupon some hideous woman who had been concealed among the trees now came forward and gave us each a little wooden bowl. The chief and his two sons and a rather ugly old man who must have been some sort of priest, were also given these bowls, but the rest of the tribe sat still and watched us.

The baskets of food were then brought round; first a handful of some sort of grain which had been roasted—called maize, I later discovered—then pieces of half-cooked flesh, very tender and sweet, and then some soft, purplish fruits with very little flavor but a vast amount of juice. We noticed that as the Indians finished they turned their bowls upside down on the ground with a peculiar twist of the wrist and most of us attempted to imitate them.

The meal appeared to be over, yet no one moved. The Indians all sat very still.

"Perhaps we're supposed to move first," muttered Ottigny. "I shall have to move soon—both my legs have got cramp."

"The pipe!" said Laudonniere out of the side of his mouth. "Wait for the pipe!"

The chief now clapped his hands and some more women came up. One carried a flat piece of wood about as big as a chair seat, and placed it on the ground before the chief. Another put a handful of large brown leaves on the board, and a third added a handful of broken tree-bark. When they had gone, the chief produced his knife and proceeded to cut first the brown leaves and then the bark into strips. He added some of the bark judiciously to the other heap, mixed it well and then unslung his tomahawk, a sort of mattock and chopper combined and began to stuff some of the mixture into a hollow place bored out of the shaft of the weapon.

The old priest, or whatever he was, fetched a burning stick from a small fire burning at the foot of the column and held it over the hollow in the tomahawk while the chief sucked hard at the end of the handle. The mixture of leaves began to smoulder and the chief sucked the smoke up the shaft and into his mouth and then blew it out into the air. This, of course, was the famous tobacco of which I had heard many travelers' tales. The Indians in the islands discovered by the Spanish explorer Columbus smoked tobacco a different way, so I have heard. They rolled the leaf into a sort of tube and putting one end of the tube to their nose breathed smoke in.

When the chief had the tobacco well alight, he passed the tomahawk round the circle and each person in turn took a suck at it and blew the smoke out his of mouth.

I noticed while the tomahawk was being passed that when the Indians blew their smoke out it formed a thin brown cloud which quickly disappeared, whereas our people produced great clouds that hung about in the still air for quite some time. From the way the Indians' chests rose and fell while they were sucking in the smoke I guessed that they were actually breathing it like air, and I determined to try it that way to see how it felt.

When the tomahawk eventually reached me I sucked

hard with my cheeks and then breathed in deeply through my nose and so carried the smoke with the air down into my chest. For a moment I felt as if the back of my throat had been scalded and all the muscles of my ribs paralyzed. For as long as it would take to count up to ten I was unable to breathe at all, and I was just beginning to fall into a panic when my chest gently relaxed and I breathed out the smoke again. It was gratifying to see that it made a thin brown cloud.

I passed the pipe on its way without comment and sat very still observing the peculiar feeling that crept over me. At first it was merely a wretched feeling of sickness. Saliva poured into my mouth so that I had to swallow continually, and my head went dizzy so that everything seemed to sway around me. Soon that cleared and I had a most delightful feeling of being raised up off the hard ground and of floating softly on a downy cushion. The woodland sounds of birds and soft talking of people came and went in my ears like the distant sound of the sea on a fitful wind. Everything I looked at appeared startling clear and beautiful, and I felt utterly content with everying and everybody and at peace with the world.

It only lasted a few minutes, though; suddenly a sharp elbow nudged me and Pierre's rather grating voice said, "Come on, we're on the move again. What on earth are you grinning at?"

"Was I grinning?" I said, coming back to the normal world with a rush and standing up a little shakily.

"You looked like a lovesick poodle," said Pierre. "Do come on."

The others were already leaving the clearing and the

Indians had all vanished—into the forest I supposed—although I certainly did not see them go. Pierre hurried me along until we had almost caught the others up, then he said to me:

"Look, I'm not very keen on this river work. Not in my line. I've got a little idea of my own I'd like to try out here. By myself, see?"

"But you're supposed to be with us," I said.

"That's right," said Pierre, patting my shoulder. "Supposed to be. But I've got other plans, see? Now, just you trot along like a good fellow and go with the rest. They won't notice I'm not there till they reach the boats and then they'll be too eager to get on to worry about me."

"They might ask me where you are," I said.

"Say you haven't seen me," said Pierre. Then, "No, that won't do. You haven't the sort of face for telling good lies. Say I turned back and you don't know where I've gone. Because you don't, you see. Thanks a lot. See you later."

And with that he gave me a final friendly pat and dodged back through the woods and was out of sight almost immediately.

As he had guessed, no one noticed his absence until we had embarked. Luckily for me I was asked no questions.

"He may have got lost in the woods," said Ottigny. "Shall I send a man back to look for him, sir?"

"Certainly not," snapped Laudonniere. "He deserves a good scare for losing sight of the party. Leave him. Cast off, there!" And off we went up the slow, wide river, eager for what we should see round the next bend.

5

Very soon the river widened out and became so shallow that the only safe channel was somewhere in the center. The whole area for miles in all directions seemed a desolation of water. Sedges and tall water plants grew up to a hundred yards from the river banks, and on our left there was no clear distinction between land and water. Many of the trees grew out of the water and drooped their leaves down to meet their reflections. Even the seemingly dry land had a dark, moist look as if it would make insecure footing for a heavy man. The only animals to be seen were the usual flocks of noisy birds and a formidable number of alligators of all sizes.

Some of these repulsive creatures were large enough to have upset our sturdy boats, and Laudonniere ordered us out into midstream to avoid them. The other boat under the more adventurous Ottigny nearly came to grief over one of these monsters. It happened in this way.

One of the alligators, an enormous one twelve or fourteen feet in length, lay basking well out into the stream and made no effort to submerge or even to swim away as we approached. A soldier in Ottigny's boat shouted that he would make the old carcass shift himself, and carefully aiming his arquebus, he fired broadside into the creature at only thirty feet range. The charge struck the alligator full in the side and rocked him in the water like an old log, but apart from that he gave no sign whatever that he had been hit.

"Draw alongside!" cried the soldier. "I'll blow his silly brains out." And he proceeded to reload with nearly a double charge of powder while the helmsman took the boat right up to the alligator which still showed no signs of moving.

Now the soldier leaned out of the boat and as the alligator was brought alongside he pressed the muzzle of his weapon against the creature's head and touched off the charge a second time. There was a roar as the overloaded weapon went off and the soldier was thrown clean over the boat and into the water on the far side. At the same time the alligator opened its huge jaws showing long rows of horrid yellow teeth and then disappeared under the water in a white flurry.

A few moments later he half appeared under the boat itself. Some of the men screamed as the stern was thrown into the air, and the alligator's tail came out of the water with the force of a running coach and crushed the gunwale in as if it had been a pie crust. For a moment we thought the boat must surely upset, but somehow it righted itself, wonderfully it seemed, almost as a dropped cat twists in the air and lands on its feet. The brave soldier was hauled back into the boat, wet and miserable, swearing that he would be revenged on the "hideous old baggage" as he called the alligator.

When, however, the alligator reappeared a few minutes later and swam slowly and insolently through the reeds towards the bank, the soldier stopped his grumbling and made no attempt to pursue it any farther. In fact, after that, Ottigny's boat followed our example and kept well out into the stream away from these dangerous creatures.

Incidentally, Le Moyne told me that according to the old Roman writers the crocodiles of the River Nile—very similar creatures to these alligators—lie on the banks with their jaws open while small birds hop in and out and peck away the morsels of food from the crevices between their teeth. I looked for such a case among the many alligators I saw on the river banks but never noticed one. Possibly the alligator is less trustworthy in temper, and the birds of Florida will not risk their lives for such a poor dinner.

After that we sailed on, continuing westward, for about five miles until we came to a large island in the middle of the river. This island stood well up above the surrounding country and was the only hill that we had so far seen. At some points the shore sloped down gently to the water, but mostly a yellow, sandy cliff face, without bushes or vegetation, formed a natural protection.

"Twenty men on that island could hold the river," said Laudonniere directly he saw it.

"And two boats on the river could hold the island," added Le Moyne. "It's a two-edged sword, that."

Laudonniere did not reply but gave the order to land and the boats drew in, coasting along a little until we struck one of the gentle slopes where we would not need to clamber about on hands and knees. The whole party went to the top of the bluff to get the first all-round picture of the country.

The first thing we noticed was that the river, which so far had been flowing from west to east, made a sudden bend not far off and stretched away to the south roughly parallel with the coast. The land inside the bend was marshy and lay in a sort of mist which grew thicker as the sun grew hotter. Northward, however, the forest ended abruptly not far from the river bank and wide green prairies opened out. A glint of water here and there showed where streams weaved about, and large herds of deer pastured without interference. It looked like good fertile land, well stocked with game.

After they had taken a brief look at the view, most of the soldiers sauntered away to find a shady spot where they could pull off their thick leather jerkins and woolen shirts and get down on the ground for a nap. Laudonniere too lay at full length near the edge of the bluff and instructed Le Moyne first to map the area and then to draw up a plan for a defensive fort to be built on the island.

Ottigny however ranged restlessly back and forth until he had seen everything the island had to show, and then he stood over Laudonniere and fidgeted impatiently.

"Sit down, man," drawled Laudonniere. "The sun is very dangerous in these parts, and a rest will do you good."

"Rest?" said Ottigny. "Let's explore first and rest afterwards."

Laudonniere laughed, lying back full length on the grass and turning his pale face up to the sky. "You're like a boy, really you are," he said at last. "You want to explore for the sake of exploring. I only needed to find a place for the first settlement, and I've found it here. Why walk about in the sun when the work is all done?"

"You call this a day's work?" said Ottigny.

"A very successful one," said Laudonniere. "Now, sit down, like a good fellow. You make me uneasy stamping about there."

Ottigny sat awkwardly on the grass, very upright and very uncomfortable. I was unpacking Le Moyne's drawing material close by and was faintly amused. However,

I was a little bored also at the thought of sitting about on the island with a whole unexplored continent in front of us.

Within five minutes Ottigny was on his feet again and wandering aimlessly about looking first into the branches of the trees and then down on to the river from the edge of the cliff. After a while he was standing behind Le Moyne watching him at work. Laudonniere was half asleep by now, and most of the soldiers entirely so. Le Moyne had finished a rough map of the area and a more detailed design for a triangular fort or camp on the high land of the island on which we were. At that point he was working with great concentration on a beautiful drawing of the mouth of the river, with two ships in the foreground and one of the boats crammed full of men sailing off upstream: it was a slightly simplified version of our departure that morning.

Eventually he became aware of Ottigny standing over him and he said mildly, "Don't stare at me, there's a good fellow. It puts me off."

"Sorry," mumbled Ottigny and moved away to come to a stop again over the dozing Laudonniere. As he stared down Laudonniere seemed to feel the stare and opened his eyes. "You still standing?" he said sleepily. "Oh, dear, it makes me quite tired just to look at you."

"Do you mind if I go off for a while?" said Ottigny abruptly.

"Off? Off where?"

"Anywhere. Just for a look round," said Ottigny.

Laudonniere's thin eyelids flickered helplessly down over his eyes again. "Go to the moon if you like," he said.

"Thank you," said Ottigny, and was four or five paces away before he had finished saying it.

"Better not go alone," added Laudonniere, and then in a mumble, "Not safe. Not safe." The words burbled away on his lips and he was asleep again.

Ottigny hesitated thoughtfully and then strode over to the main clump of trees under which the soldiers were lying.

"Now then," he said cheerfully, "anyone feel like a nice little walk into the woods?"

One or two of the soldiers opened their eyes to stare at him and then they rolled over on their sides away from him with wordless grunts. One muttered, "Have a heart." Another, a young trumpeter, said cheekily, "Is that an order, sir?"

"No, blast you, it's not an order," snapped Ottigny. "Sleep your brains into a pudding if you want to. No one will notice the difference anyway."

He was on the point of turning angrily away when a voice I recognized as Red's floated out of the air.

"May I come, sir?"

"And who the blazes are you?" demanded Ottigny looking wildly around.

There was a rustle in one of the trees, and Red dropped from a branch to the ground. "Me, sir."

"I'd be glad of your company," said Ottigny kindly. "Come along then, if you're ready."

"I think Pierre would like to come, too," said Red seeing me hovering in the background.

"Pierre? Oh, another boy. Why didn't you speak up for yourself, lad?"

"I thought you wanted some of the men with you," I said. "I didn't like to push myself forward."

"I'd sooner have two eager lads than twenty corpses," said Ottigny contemptuously. "Are you both armed?"

Even on this expedition boys were not allowed to carry swords, and the arquebuses were only issued to the soldiers.

"I've a crossbow," said Red.

"Are you good with it?"

"Reasonably."

"It'll do. Fetch it and hurry," said Ottigny.

A few minutes later the three of us were scrambling down to the river's edge. Fortunately the sailors were awake and carried us up the river without much delay. Ottigny had decided that the southern bank would be too marshy and the flat plains to the north too dull, so we went west to where the river curved, and landed on the farther bank. Here the forest was thick and shady, but not too thick for us to move freely about in. With a quick glance at the lie of the river and the angle of the sun, Ottigny led the way straight into the woods and we hopped along after him talking excitedly and on the alert for any wonders that might show themselves.

But except for the general wonder of being in a new world, we discovered very little that we had not already seen. There were the birds, of course, all about us in great numbers, and we were continually startling deer like the one Arlac had shot. Often these deer went along in the forest keeping pace with us only a short distance away in the trees, and they showed very little fear. We discovered later that many of the Indian tribes fed and encouraged the deer to stay close to the camps so that they would always be on hand for meat. And as their method of killing was with the bow and arrow, silent and unobvious, the creatures stayed on in the neighborhood without fear.

We saw in one place a huge tree with grayish trunk and thin shiny leaves covered with small caterpillars to such an extent that their movement gave the foliage a strange rippling appearance. The cocoons of these caterpillars were covered in fine yellow silk, and Ottigny believed them to be a sort of silkworm native to the place. As we never saw an Indian dressed in silk, I assumed that they had not discovered the art of spinning silk from the cocoons or of weaving cloth.

After an hour or more of tramping through the forest we grew disappointed with our little exploration, and Red and I would willingly have turned back. Ottigny, however, still plodded on as if, having made the effort to begin, he would not now stop until he had found something new to report to Laudonniere. Suddenly the forest ended with a thick belt of laurel trees and gave on to an area of marsh. It was choked and overgrown with weeds and rushes that grew in such a tangle, the living and dead together, that it would have been impossible to make any progress through it. Ottigny did advance a few yards, hacking at the growth with his sword, but he sank to the knees in a vile smelling black sludge and eventually gave up and struggled back to us.

"Well, that's that," he said. "We can go no farther, so we might as well rest here and then go back. Perhaps if we bear off a little to the right or left we may strike something new."

We had brought no food or drink with us so there was

nothing for it but to sit glumly on the ground under one of the larger laurels and stare at one another. The laurels kept off the heat of the sun admirably, and also cut off any view into the surrounding forest. It was rather like sitting in a large, green, badly-lit room without the benefit of furniture.

We had only been seated a short while, and I was glancing idly at this wall of green, when my eyes fell with amazement on a brown head poking out between the leaves. Near it was another, and yet another: five in all. The heads did not move, but all the eyes stared straight at me. For one absurd moment I thought the heads were the flowers of this strange foreign laurel tree, and then one of the heads blinked its eyelids. I was too amazed to say anything but I raised one hand and pointed.

Ottigny showed no surprise. He merely stood up and spoke to them in a gentle and persuasive voice, asking them to come forward if they were friendly to us, and when he had finished the leaves parted and five very ordinary Indians came out into the open. Their heads were fixed on their shoulders in the normal way, and I think I was a little disappointed, though what I had expected I can't now imagine.

These Indians, after inspecting us curiously and touching our clothes and skins—and I suppose we seemed as outlandish to them as they did to us—appeared to want to take us somewhere; probably to their village. Ottigny and Red were eager to go with them so I was forced to hide my own nervousness in case they should ridicule me. I am rather cautious by nature and like to look before I leap, but sometimes others mistake this for cowardice and mock me for it.

In any case the Indians led us to the edge of the reedy swamp where we had been forced to turn back and there they made signs to show that they wanted us to climb on the backs of the three sturdiest of them and be carried across the marsh. We did as they asked, making jokes to one another about our peculiar steeds, and the Indians grinned at our gaiety and plunged into the mud.

There must have been some concealed path through the swamp which the Indians knew well. They doubled and twisted here and there among great tangled clumps of rushes and marsh weed, almost up to the knees in black liquid mud but never for a moment hesitating as to where to go. The marsh bubbled and oozed as they trod through it, and gave off a most vile stink which at first made me feel quite sick and dizzy. After a while, however, it had much the same effect as strong wine; I became lightheaded and began to cry out all kinds of nonsense and even burst into snatches of song. The Indians seemed not to be affected but the other two were acting in a very peculiar way so that when eventually we reached the hard earth once more and were set down less than twenty yards from a small group of round, thatched Indian huts we were quite stupid from this marsh gas and could scarcely walk straight without assistance.

I am glad to say we had completely recovered by the time we reached the huts and the chief who stood up to welcome us.

It was not a very large village; seven or eight of these round huts which meant a population of about fifty people of all ages. It was built on a small raised bump in the middle of the marsh, and was, we supposed, safe from attack on that account. On the other hand it was also a long way from any tracts of fertile ground, so that this particular little tribe clearly did not do any farming. There were poles stuck up here and there in the camp hung with the bodies of marsh birds, eels and in only one case a small deer, so we gathered that these must be the tribe's larders and that the people lived pretty much on what they could catch in the surrounding swamps. How they managed to survive the winter I could not tell.

While we were gazing around the chief came up to welcome us. He was a very old man, shriveled in flesh with hardly a thumb's space on his skin not crisscrossed with tiny wrinkles. His long white hair, sadly tinged with green at the ends, hung down on his chest and reached below his waist.

A young and pretty girl came out of the hut behind him carrying a handsome cape of shining gray feathers, probably of the heron, and put it over his shoulders. This was perhaps his ceremonial costume, for the other Indians wore nothing but the usual leather apron gathered up over the hips and hanging well down in front.

When the old man had touched us and satisfied his curiosity about us he sat down cross-legged on the ground and called something aloud to the people behind him. One of them went into a hut and brought four earthenware bowls of about pint size and handed one to each of us.

"The welcoming feast," whispered Red. "I can do with it, too." None of us had eaten since the morning, and we were feeling extremely hungry.

After a wait of a few minutes another Indian came forward with a rough clay jar and very carefully, and with immense ceremony, poured about a quarter of a pint of water into each bowl. There was a sort of sigh from the watching Indians as this was done.

"If this is the soup," I said, "it's very weak."

The chief raised his bowl and took a small sip of the water. He smacked his lips loudly and looked at us over the rim of his bowl as we drank.

"Fresh spring water," said Ottigny. "They must go miles to get this. We'd better make a fuss about it—they're probably doing us a great honor or something."

So the three of us drank our bowls of plain water as noisily as we could, nodding and winking at one another and making as much fuss as jugglers at a fair. It seemed to satisfy the Indians who broke into excited talk among themselves.

At this point the ceremony was interrupted by a slight disturbance behind the crowd, and two tall young men came forward carrying a sort of litter or bed on which lay an incredibly old man. His white hair lay thickly over him like a cover, and out of it poked a thin dried face so still and brittle that it might have been molded out of paper. His eyelids were closed and at first we thought he was a mummified corpse.

The villagers drew back with obvious respect to allow the procession through, and the bed was set down in front of us. For a moment there was no movement anywhere. The Indians watched the old man's face, and we waited to be told what it was all about. Only two young eagles, in their fluffy first year's plumage edged up and down on the bar above the old man's head. Their wings were bound down to their sides with leather thongs but they were unhooded and their feet were free.

One of these eagles, which had been staring at us

angrily out of wide yellow eyes, suddenly gaped and uttered a shrill scream. The old man's eyes flickered and opened and he stared around him for a while until he discovered us strangers. The chief drew us forward to the side of the bed so that the old man could inspect us, and this he did for some time through gray, clouded eyes. His expression did not change. Finally he slowly opened his lips and uttered a few short sentences in a hoarse whisper the effort of which seemed to exhaust him, for he closed his eyes again immediately after and kept them closed.

Apparently he approved of us, for the chief then lifted the two young eagles and gave them to Red and me as presents. The birds did not seem very pleased about the exchange, but we spoke to them and stroked them and after a time they calmed down and settled contentedly on our wrists.

"Do you think we can train them?" I asked Red.

"I don't know," he said, "but I'm going to have a good try." Back in France, of course, it would have been quite illegal for us to own eagles, let alone try to use them for hawking. Only a lord or a baron was permitted to use such majestic birds. But here it was different.

We made the customary return presents: I a leather pouch and Red a small knife; and the chief appeared well pleased with the exchange.

Just before we left he took us to a carved and painted post that stood in the doorway of the old man's hut and showed us certain markings which ran all the way down the post on two sides. We gathered that it was a sort of calender of the old man's life, and that each mark represented a month. The marks were grouped in fours, so that it was easy to count off the years, and from it I gathered that the old man was two hundred and thirty years old. This was hard to believe, and yet I could see no other way of calculating, so in the end we accepted it and went away wondering.

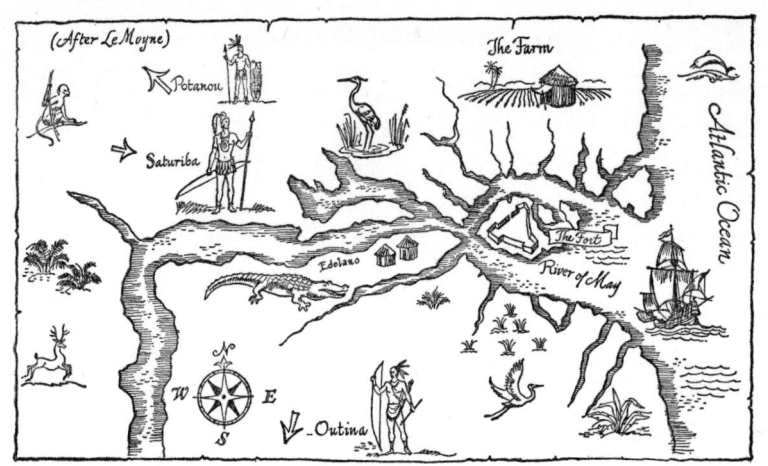

Chapter Three

THE FORT

WITHOUT ANY waste of time Laudonniere made arrangements for the building of the settlement. Early next morning—the day after our little exploration up the river—he gave orders that the two smaller ships should be towed across the sand bars at the mouth of the river and thence upstream as far as possible towards the island he had chosen for a fort. The third and largest ship was to remain at the old moorings with ten soldiers and a crew of seven to guard the entrance. Two cannons from each of the other ships were transferred in order to give her greater strength and firepower should the necessity arise. All the rest of the party were to proceed up the river.

Laudonniere also very cleverly ordered the malcontents of the previous day to make a landing on the south bank of the river and go upstream on foot. This meant they could make no further complaint about not being allowed to land, and it also lightened the ship so that they drew less water and would be easier to tow over the bars. Those of us who knew what sort of country lay along the south bank got a sly delight in thinking of the obnoxious Fourneaux toiling through five miles of marsh while we did the journey in comfort by water.

But after the shore party was landed and the necessary exchanges made between the ships, it was found that the sand bars were much higher than had been thought, and that neither of the smaller ships could be drawn up the river. So the whole party had to make a landing on the south bank and leave the carpenters and the engineers to bring the building material and equipment up in the two small sailing boats.

By the time all this had been done and the landing completed it was well into the heat of the day. Tempers were frayed and when we eventually moved off into the forest it was in a very disgruntled frame of mind.

Laudonniere as the leader of the expedition, and because by now he had a good idea of the lie of the land, went ahead with Le Moyne and half a dozen soldiers under Arlac to cut tracks where necessary and to act as an advance guard. The rest of the settlers followed in a huge undisciplined crowd, the packs and bundles of their personal possessions on their shoulders. They kept no march discipline at all and were forever straying off in groups into the forest and getting lost.

Ottigny and La Caille brought up the rear with the rest of the soldiers and attempted to urge forward the slow ones and bring back to the path those who persistently wandered off in the wrong direction. I was with

Laudonniere and Le Moyne in the front, and Red and Pierre, I thought, were with Ottigny. We did not see one another until late in the afternoon when Laudonniere called a halt and gathered the party together.

The march was more wearing than we had thought it would be. Laudonniere had led us well to the south to avoid the marshes that lay along the river bank, but the marshes were bigger than he had thought, and the detour turned into an afternoon's hard struggle through tangled jungle and soft, treacherous semi-bog. We covered eight or nine miles and were still not sure of how far we had to go.

At last, as the sun began to sink below the treetops, we came to a huge glade. Short grass and cool moss stretched in smooth curves for about two hundred yards in every direction. Dotted about the glade were great flowering trees with trunks big enough for three men to hold hands round. A small stream of clear, sweet water ran across this glade and much game moved on the edge of the forest. It was an ideal place to pause and gather our forces.

Laudonniere gave the order to rest. Some of the soldiers took the opportunity of going off into the wood, hunting, and soon the sharp sounds of their arquebuses came from among the trees. These noises served the double purpose of getting food for supper and giving stragglers an idea of where we were to be found.

About an hour later Ottigny and La Caille and the rear party came up with us. By this time the soldiers had built half a dozen large fires, and the carcasses of a number of deer were being jointed and fixed on primitive spits for roasting. The heat had suddenly gone out of the day, and although there was still a good light it would not last much longer.

Laudonniere welcomed Ottigny and together they went about the glade counting, through the drifting clouds of woodsmoke, those who had arrived. I found Red lying on his back on a heap of dead leaves, too tired to take off his equipment or get himself meat.

"A hard day?" I said.

"Hard? My faith, it was hard," he said. "The stupidity of some people is difficult to believe. All I've been doing is running back and forth, back and forth like a hunting dog, fetching people back to the track, helping them out of bogs and ditches, trying to persuade them to keep up with the party for their own sakes. I must have done three yards to everyone else's one. And La Caille would keep saying, 'Your legs are younger than mine. Just run over and fetch in those fools there.' In the end it got past a joke."

"I don't suppose that suited Pierre," I laughed. "He's not fond of hard work?"

"Pierre? I've not seen him all day," said Red. "Surely he was with you?"

"No," I said. "I've not seen him either. That's very strange. Do you think he can have got lost?"

Red laughed. "I think Pierre can be trusted to look after himself."

But all the same I was worried about our friend. I had not had a chance of finding out what he had done with himself the day before when he had dodged the expedition upriver. I had a feeling that he was trying to avoid us and that he had something secret up his sleeve. In any case I thought his absence ought to be reported to

Laudonniere, as Pierre might have got into danger somewhere out in the forest. I got up and went to look for Laudonniere.

When I came up with him, however, I said nothing about Pierre after all because I was just in time to hear him saying furiously to his lieutenant:

"Fifty-seven gone astray! My God, I've a good mind to make an example of the lot of them."

"Many are noblemen," said Ottigny

"I don't care if they're bishops," stormed Laudonniere. "While I'm leader here they are all under my command, and they must obey orders."

Ottigny laughed shortly. "I'm afraid that's something they're not very good at," he said

"Then they must learn," snapped Laudonniere. "And what's more, from now on I'll see that they do. As they find their way into camp, send them to me!"

"Very good, sir," said Ottigny with military smartness. "We stay here the night, then?"

"Yes. And we'll have the trumpeter blow a call at dawn tomorrow and make an early start."

Ottigny was about to turn away when a thought struck him. "Don't you think we had better send out a few search parties for the missing?" he said.

"Certainly not," said Laudonniere, looking furious.

"But suppose they don't find the camp, sir?"

"Let them starve in the forest. Better men have come to worse ends."

I felt that it was no time to mention Pierre's absence and making some trivial excuse I got away and went back to Red.

All the missing people except Pierre found the camp

before night fell, and were sent on arrival to Laudonniere's. I don't know what he said to them but they all looked very shamefaced about the affair. Laudonniere in one of his rages could be very frightening.

Pierre did not arrive in the camp either that night or the next morning. Red persuaded me to say nothing about it.

"Laudonniere's in a mood to hang the next person to disobey an order," he pointed out, "and he might well pick on Pierre and make an example of him."

"But he may be lost and starving—perhaps dying of a wound," I said.

"Even that's better than being hanged," said Red. "And anyway, I shouldn't worry too much about our self-confident friend. I don't doubt he'll turn up smiling before very long."

The camp was roused at dawn by the trumpeter, and the march recommenced before the sun was above the trees. As it turned out we were nearer to our destination than anyone had suspected, and we broke out of the forest onto the open river bank after we had been going about an hour.

The place that had been chosen for the settlement was within sight downstream, and we had only overshot it by half a mile or so.

The carpenters and engineers were already encamped on the top of the hill, having reached it the previous afternoon. All the gear had been landed, and one of the carpenters—old Chabrier—had even been through the edges of the forest blazing marks on the straightest of the pine trees which he had picked out for use on the fort. Fourneaux and the rest of his party, who had traveled in advance of us, were nowhere to be seen.

"We heard some shots away out back there," said Chabrier. "We thought it would be some of you coming up."

"What time was this?" asked La Caille.

"Just about noon yesterday," said Chabrier. "Wasn't so far away, either. But we were busy and didn't want to interrupt our work to go ferreting around in the woods...."

"Of course, not," said La Caille quickly. Chabrier was an old countryman who was fond of explaining things in great detail, wearying his hearers with trivial and uncalled-for stories.

"Or could it have been a bit later," added Chabrier thoughtfully. "We had a bite to eat at noon and then I remember I had a look over the axes to see if any needed sharpening—and a good job I did, for some of them were in a sorry way. Some of these youngsters didn't ought to be allowed to use a good ax, the damage they cause by their thoughtlessness...."

"And that's when you heard the shots?" asked La Caille, trying to keep the old man to his story.

"No, I was just coming to that. I sorted out these axes as I said and then there were three needing attention. So I said to Joseph, I said, 'Just you look at these,' I said. 'Did you ever see such a neglectment of good steel?' I said. And Joseph, he took a look and he said..."

"So you sharpened them," prodded La Caille.

"Indeed, I didn't," said Chabrier, very annoyed. "I'm a master carpenter, and sharpening's not my business."

And so the conversation went on until La Caille at last

established that the shots had certainly occurred long before our little advance party had gone after deer. The question was, how could Fourneaux's party have got so close to their destination and then lost themselves in the last quarter mile?

Laudonniere, however, seemed quite unperturbed about the affair. Apart from muttering something about Fourneaux's loss being "a good riddance to bad rubbish," he dismissed the business with a wave of his hand. "The important thing," he cried, "is to get the fort built. After that we can feel secure enough to attend to smaller matters."

And with that he set to with tremendous energy to organize the settlers into parties under one or other of technical experts for work with the building.

It was at this point, when the men were being divided up into parties for tree felling, carting, digging, carrying, building, that I suddenly realized what a queer lopsided bunch these settlers were. To be truthful, it was Red who put the idea into my mind. Laudonniere was selecting his groups by the simple method of asking each man in turn what his trade had been before, and according to the answer and the man's strength, so he gave him his job.

"Do you notice," whispered Red to me while this was going on, "how few of them have ever done any real work? Work with their hands, I mean."

"No," I said. "But what do you mean, exactly?"

"Listen!"

Laudonniere was just approaching a small group of a dozen or so men who were waiting to be allotted to their work parties.

"Trade?" he said to the first man.

"Shopkeeper."
"Can you handle an ax?"
"After a fashion."
"Tree-felling party, then. Over there with Joseph Flac. And you?"
"Me?"
"Yes, you. Occupation?"
"None," said the man proudly. (He meant that he was a nobleman, of course.)
"Printer," said another.
"Shopkeeper."
"Merchant."
"None."
"None."
"Clerk."
"Shopkeeper."
"Soldier."
"Weaver."

So they each answered in turn and were given jobs. Few had ever handled an ax or mattock, and none claimed any knowledge of building. Laudonniere passed on to us.

"Printer," said I.
"Farm worker," said Red.

Laudonniere stopped suddenly. "What?" he asked, looking incredulous.

"Farm worker."

"That makes two of you in more than four hundred settlers. Like the Israelites, we are trying to make bricks without straw."

When he had moved on, Red said, "You see what I mean? A new settlement in a new land, and the people are all noblemen or shopkeepers. There are no courts or shops here; only empty land waiting to be farmed. How shall we keep ourselves alive unless we grow food and so make our own little society? We can't live for ever on deer's flesh and forest fruits."

"Perhaps," I said, "we shall obtain it from the Indians. They seem to have plenty."

"That's just what I fear," said Red.

We talked about it no more just then, for we had been given work to do and we went off to do it.

2

Work had been proceeding on the fort for four days. The ground had been cleared and flattened. Huge piles of trimmed timber were beginning to grow around the edges of the camp. A sort of ramp or earth wall surrounded the triangular fort area. The work was hard, and we all went gratefully to bed soon after sunset and slept heavily. Laudonniere drove us hard, never seeming to need rest himself and grudging it to others.

Fourneaux and his party had still not appeared, and neither had Pierre Gambi. Fortunately Laudonniere seemed to think that he had sent Pierre with Fourneaux and so made no special comment on his absence. He put all the blame on Fourneaux himself whom he considered to be a troublemaker.

By the end of the fourth day the various work parties had got used to the tasks they had been set and everything went very smoothly. Arlac, with five or six of the soldiers—the best shots—had been made responsible for feeding us, and they went out daily at dawn either to hunt in the forest or to make contact with Indian villages and trade with the natives for corn, pumpkins or beans. The food this party obtained by hunting or trading, by begging and sometimes, I fear, by stealing, was shared out equally. It supplemented the daily ration issued by Laudonniere from his stores, this being one glass of neat spirits, a handful of dried peas or beans, cheese or salt meat and a large pinch of salt. From the two sources of supply we fed well and kept up our energy for the hard work we were doing.

On the afternoon of the fourth day Red and I were working on the main gate of the fort, ramming earth around the two great posts. A causeway from the island to the north bank of the river had just been finished, and it was no longer necessary to use a boat from the fort to the fertile plains where most of the Indian villages were. Arlac and his party came in through the gateway as Red and I were finishing our job and clearing up.

"I've got news for you two," he called.

"Good news?" I asked.

Arlac waited until the soldiers with him had passed into the fort carrying the baskets of Indian corn, fruit and lizard's flesh they had collected during the day.

"We've been a bit farther afield today," he said. "Got as far as the village of the great chief himself."

"Saturiba?" I said. "What's he like?"

"We didn't see him. He kept out of sight inside his hut and dealt with us through his headman and an interpreter. And you'll never guess *who* the interpreter was!"

"Pierre Gambi!" said Red and I together.

Arlac laughed. "Right the first time," he said. "And it would have given you a laugh to see him there, squatting on a heap of robes and bossing everyone about. Saturiba seems very pleased with him, though the two sons were whispering away in a corner with faces like a couple of bowls of sour milk."

"But what is Pierre doing there?"

"Bless me, I don't know," said Arlac. "I didn't get a chance to talk with him alone. But I'll tell you one thing: he has learned the language these people speak. Jabbering away to them, he was, fifteen to the dozen. Not like La Caille with his one or two words of Indian talk and then a lot of hand waving to fill in the gaps. No, young Pierre's really picked it up. How he's done it in the time, Heaven alone knows."

"He can be very quick when it's to his advantage," I said, and then, as Red frowned at me, I realized that I had been guilty of disloyalty to our friend.

"It's a very good thing in one way," went on Arlac. "It made it easy to do business. We just told young Pierre what we had come for and he had it fixed up with the chief in no time at all. He's a smart lad, I reckon. Whether we like it or not we're going to depend for a long time on the good will of these Indians, and young Gambi's going to be a great help in making sure we don't fall out with them through some stupid misunderstanding. I say, good luck to him."

Arlac went on his way into the fort, grinning to himself. Red and I, however, were not so amused. It was obvious what game Pierre was playing, but we both felt that he might have been a shade too clever this time. An interpreter was a very useful thing to have, but unless Laudonniere had given his permission—and I was fairly certain that he had not—he was the sort of man to feel anything but pleased at Pierre's independent action.

"I wonder if we'd better see Laudonniere and get our word in first," I said.

"He's bound to hear," agreed Red. "Arlac's so struck with it that he's bound to tell everyone. And then the fat will be in the fire."

But before we could make up our minds which way to act, a tremendous hubbub burst out in the unfinished fort. Trumpets sounded the alarm, men shouted, officers called orders and from every direction settlers came running. It was the general alarm that had been sounded. Every man was supposed to take up a position of defence behind the earth rampart and be prepared to repel an Indian attack.

Our place was by the main gate so we had only to drop our rammers and pick up our bows to be ready. Inside two minutes everyone was in his allotted place and absolute silence lay over the fort. Laudonniere had climbed to the roof of the two-story building that was to be his headquarters when it was finished, and was staring out northward over the forest. After a while he climbed slowly down again and walked across the open towards us, Ottigny with him but a respectful pace to the rear. Nothing moved but these two, threading their way between piles of sawn timber and half-dug foundations.

The main gate had been lowered into position and four men were dragging the bars through the slots behind it. Red and I stood just outside the fort on the beginning of the causeway. Our job was to defend the two ship's gunners who were frantically loading and priming one of the three cannons mounted in the fort. They were loading the chain; enough to clear the causeway if it were rushed. Behind us—and I kept glancing over my shoulder to be sure of this—was our escape hole, a gap in the timber defences about two feet wide and four feet high, and it was through this hole that I saw Laudonniere and Ottigny approach the gate.

When they were still a few yards off, Laudonniere cried out, "Raise the gate! But keep your eyes on the forest."

The bars clattered out, the gate creaked slowly up, and Laudonniere and Ottigny came out on to the causeway and stood there beside us looking into the still green across the river. Nothing moved there except a long-legged white bird moving solemnly along the edge of the water, turning the stones with its bill.

"It's not a massed attack," Laudonniere said quietly to Ottigny. "The party I saw approaching was no more than fifty or sixty strong."

"There may be others concealed."

"They were not dressed for war," said Laudonniere. "These Indians do not use that sort of deception in their warfare."

"Do they use deception at all?" asked Ottigny.

"I don't believe they do. They are a very honest and simple people," said Laudonniere thoughtfully. "If they do turn dishonest it will be because they have learned the art from the Spaniard."

"Or from the French," said Ottigny.

"We have not been here long enough," said Laudonniere cynically.

At that point a party of Indians came out from the trees on the far bank and advanced to the end of the causeway. One of the gunners, blowing his match into a brighter glow, looked up inquiringly.

"Do nothing until you are ordered," said Laudonniere, catching the man's action. Then he walked forward, a few paces in front of the cannon, and called out to the Indians in their own language.

After a little hubbub of discussion, two of the Indians came along the causeway while the remainder squatted down to wait. When the deputation reached us they saluted and crouched down also. Laudonniere hesitated and then went down on his haunches in an imitation of them. They began to talk, with much waving behind them to the forest and much mentioning of Saturiba.

"All the same," whispered Red, "they don't seem to be getting anywhere. They need our little Pierre to help them."

Laudonniere seemed to have come to a similar conclusion for he now called over his shoulder, "Fetch La Caille, one of you. At the double!"

Red and I both raced for the gap in the wall and he beat me to it by a couple of paces. I let him go. He returned with La Caille in a few minutes and the palaver with the Indians began again. La Caille too seemed to be having difficulty but in the end he said to Laudonniere:

"Can't say that I'm certain what they mean, but it seems to be about a visit from Saturiba. They say the great chief comes to speak with the white men and see their dwelling places."

"I gathered something of the sort," said Laudonniere. "But then there is something about a house for the chief. Do they mean Saturiba wants to move into the fort? That would be a nuisance, and no mistake."

La Caille turned back to the Indians and questioned them for some time. "I've got it," he cried at last. "It's some sort of state visit, and these people have been sent on before to make some sort of preparation. I think they want to build a conference hut or some such place, so that the two of you can meet in privacy on neutral ground, as it were."

Laudonniere laughed. "Well, they could certainly give the King of France a few points on ceremonial courtesy," he said.

"Shall I give them permission, then?"

"By all means. So long as their hut is outside the fort."

The Indians seemed well pleased with the answer La Caille gave them and went off back to their friends on the river bank. Laudonniere ordered every one back to work inside the fort with the exception of the gun crews who were to keep alert for any treachery, and Red and myself who were to observe carefully what the party of Indians did and report every so often to Ottigny or to Laudonniere himself.

For the next hour or so, Red and I stood by the main gateway growing more and more bored with staring at the edge of the forest. The Indians had disappeared and the forest seemed unnaturally quiet. The sun was extremely hot and tiresome, and it was all we could do to keep each other awake.

At last, however, the Indians came out of the forest again, a little way down from the end of the causeway. This time they carried long curved knives dangling by a thong from their waist belts, and most of them were loaded with bundles of thin rods, flat leaves, Spanish moss or coils of a rough sort of vegetable rope.

In a desultory sort of way they began to cut saplings and trim them into lengths of ten or twelve feet. There seemed to be no great hurry among them, and from this we concluded that Saturiba was not intending to visit for some time yet, certainly not before the next day. Every now and then one or another of the Indians would stray away from the others and begin to hunt for birds' eggs among the pebbles of the river bank, or lie down for a rest in the shade. No one seemed to mind. At one time there was only one rather elderly man left on the building site and all he was doing was to walk solemnly round and round on a small circle, stamping with his feet and crooning a quiet song to himself. We guessed that he was preparing the floor of the hut, making a smooth, hard, almost polished surface on the bare earth by the constant pressure of his feet.

Just before dark the Indians cleared up their tools and went off into the forest again, evidently finished for the day, and we were able to go off and report to Laudonniere what they had so far accomplished. He did not seem at all surprised at their slowness.

"It'll probably be a week or more before Saturiba desides to come," he said. "In fact I shouldn't be at all surprised if he didn't forget the whole thing. They have a very imperfect idea of time, these Indians. Still, keep an eye on them for a while."

"It's a bit dull standing about watching," said Red. "Do you think we could go across and give them a hand? I'd like to see the way they do their huts; you can never tell when it might come in useful."

Laudonniere laughed. "By all means," he said. "If

they'll have you. But don't try and boss them about, will you?"

"I want to learn," said Red indignantly.

Laudonniere looked at him with obvious disbelief. "A rare quality in the young, I find," he said dryly. "The younger generation nowadays always seem to know everything—or think they do. However...."

In any case, the next morning when the Indians appeared again on the river bank, Red and I went across the causeway and squatted down fairly near to where they were working. For a few minutes they stared at us curiously, but when we merely smiled and nodded they must have decided that we were harmless and went on with their work as if we did not exist.

They cut down ten trees of about six inches diameter and began to set them up in a circle around the beaten patch of earth that had been prepared on the previous day. When three or four of the posts had been erected in this way Red said, "We could try our hand at that, anyway. It's what we've been doing over in the fort. Come on."

He got to his feet and with me close behind went over to the group of Indians stamping down the ground by each pole. They stopped immediately and looked at us with quite blank expressions, no hostility, no friendliness, nothing; just waiting.

"May we?" said Red gently, and putting one hand to a pole he began to heel the earth in around it. He kept circling the pole, holding it and pressing down the earth inch by inch. The Indians made no move for a while, and then as Red began to go round the pole for the second time they suddenly broke into exclamations of what sounded like disapproval. One of them came forward and placing a hand on Red's shoulder stopped him.

"Don't want any help?" said Red.

The Indian pointed up at the sky, in the direction of the sun. Then he moved his finger over in a wide arc, showing the direction the sun would take during the day.

"I don't understand him," Red said. "Does he mean they're going to work all day?"

The Indian took no notice. He pointed his finger again across the sky, and then with a sweeping movement he brought the end of the arc down to the foot of the pole and described a circle round it in the same direction. Red still looked puzzled. Another Indian came forward and moved Red bodily round the pole a few inches in the same direction as the sun's movement.

"He means you're going round the wrong way," I suggested.

"What difference does that make?" laughed Red.

"I don't know," I said. "Try it the other way and see how they take it."

So Red began to tread in the earth again, but this time going in the sunwise direction. The Indians smiled and patted him on the shoulder, obviously well pleased. For the rest of the day they accepted us quite naturally as members of the team, giving us jobs to do, showing us how to do them and then leaving us to carry on by ourselves. We learned how to weave Spanish moss into a curtain almost as fine as lace and hang it around the sides of the hut to take off the heat of the sun without cutting out too much light. We learned how to lay the broad palm leaves in an intricate fashion over the roof so that the slight serrations of the edges of the leaves caught in one another and made the roof flat and waterproof. And they taught us also that the man who makes the most fuss is not always doing the most work. Watching from the other side of the river the day before we had thought they were taking it very easily, getting very little done. Now we found that their way of working was deceptive. They never appeared to be working hard or fast and yet the job got done without fuss or bother, and Red and I found out to our humiliation that we did by far the smallest share.

By sunset the hut was finished. It was a large, imposing hut by Indian standards; open at the front, which faced the fort and the river, oval in shape, with curtained walls, the earth floor beaten a smooth, polished gray so that it looked and felt like a sheet of gun metal. There was room for a hundred people at least to meet inside without touching one another.

When the last touches had been made to the building, the Indians packed up their tools and quietly wandered off into the jungle. Red and I returned to the fort and told Laudonniere what had been happening.

"Finished?" he said with surprise. "I didn't expect anything as fast as that. I wonder if that means Saturiba is already on his way? Oh, well, he won't travel in the dark. We shall have to keep a sharp lookout tomorrow to give him a proper welcome."

3

Saturiba arrived the next day in the middle of the morning. There was not the slightest chance that we might have missed him for he came with all the pomp imaginable. We heard his party coming through the forest long before we saw anything. A weird howling and shrieking noise came through the trees and made every man drop the tool he was working with to listen. It was not the sound of human or animal voices, yet neither was it, to our ears, music, though there was something of music in it.

We did not have to wait for very long to see the cause of the noise. Almost immediately, as the sound became almost unbearably loud, a party of twenty or so young men came from among the trees and spread out in a line on the bank of the river just above the causeway. Each man had some sort of pipe made from hollow cane, and across the top of this he blew as loudly and as often as he could manage. This orchestra—and that, no doubt, was what it was supposed to be—shrieked on for three or four minutes and then stopped abruptly so that the air, emptied suddenly of all sound, seemed to throb like a poisoned finger.

All the settlers had crowded to the wall of the fort nearest to the procession. Ottigny dragged a few soldiers down and sent them off to guard against surprise from the other side, but I noticed that even they slunk back later to watch the fun. What would have happened had the Indians been evilly disposed and planned to attack us, I cannot think.

Next a party of armed men came silently out of the forest. They were a magnificent sight; all men of great strength and muscular development, their muscles rippling and sliding under their brown skins as they came forward at a quick, noiseless trot. There were fifty of them at least, and they made no more noise between them than does a single snake moving through the grass.

They were armed with long throwing spears—each man carried two—and rawhide shields the fronts of which were patterned intricately with white clay. As they reached the hut which we had helped to build the day before, they fanned out into a wide circle and then stood with their backs to the hut, leaning with folded arms on the tops of their shields as if their task was done.

There was another burst of discordant music from the pipers and then the main body of Saturiba's army emerged from the forest. These came quietly but in disorder, breaking through the trees at several places along the river bank and forming into an untidy line. The music grew louder and more insistent and then suddenly stopped again as Saturiba, with four attendants, appeared and paced with great dignity down the line of warriors towards the hut.

Saturiba himself was an impressive sight. He was well above the average height of the Indians of those parts, a broad manly figure with shoulders that indicated immense strength. The whole of the front of him, chest, abdomen, legs and arms, was painted with an intricate design of curls and mazes in three or four bright colors. As he came level with where Red and I were standing and then passed, I was reminded of one of those pasteboard playing cards: the brightly drawn picture of a king on one side, and on the other a dull uniform brown. The back view of the great Indian king looked a little ridiculous and insignificant after the imposing show of the front view.

Close behind the king came an old man, lame in one leg and much bent with age. He wore a huge collection of bones and dried herbs in garlands round his neck, and on his head the mask and horns of a deer so arranged as to face backwards. He was smeared from head to foot in a sort of white clay which had dried in strange cracks and ridges so that he looked, not like a man, but like a decayed fragment of tree walking. He was helped along by two tall young men who carried long, intricately carved clubs instead of the usual throwing spears. This was to indicate their royal blood, and in fact they were the sons of the king, as we discovered later.

The last of the royal party, an undersized fellow dressed in the native fashion with tasseled skirt, clay in his hair and the rest of it, walked with such a familiar swagger that I turned quickly to Red to see if he had also noticed. He was smiling slightly to himself and nodded when I looked at him.

"Pierre Gambi," he whispered. "Would you believe it? And the fun he's having."

"He's making himself quite ridiculous," I said.

"Oh, I don't know," murmured Red tolerantly. "And he has such a weakness for queer clothes.... I wonder how Laudonniere will take it."

The little procession continued along the river bank until it reached the end of the causeway, where it halted. Saturiba turned to face the fort with great dignity, his body and head erect, the corners of his mouth turned down in an expression of intense determination. Pierre came forward and stood beside him for a few moments, apparently receiving instructions, and then stepped a few paces in front on to the causeway itself.

"The great chief, Saturiba," he cried out, and his voice sounded strangely thin and bodiless like the cry of a sea bird, "sends his greetings to the people of the sun and desires to speak with their leader."

Laudonniere replied immediately, "Let him enter the fort with twelve men as our guest. The chief and I are friends, and will speak together as friends and without suspicion."

After a short consultation with Saturiba, Pierre called out, "The chief is happy to be your friend and will enter the fort gladly and with confidence. But first, he brings prisoners under guard against whom he would complain."

Laudonniere, with a quick tug at Ottigny's sleeve, strode out of the gate and out along the causeway before Pierre had finished. "What prisoners has Saturiba taken?" he cried out in an angry voice. "Has he dared to lay hands on men under my command?"

Laudonniere, with Ottigny close behind him, went forward until he was face to face with the Indian chief and the discussion was continued too far away for us to hear. After a few moments, however, Saturiba waved his hand to the men gathered around the hut, and some of them went off into the woods. When they returned a few minutes later, they were leading twenty or so prisoners, their clothing in rags about them and their arms pinioned behind with ropes.

"Fourneaux, as I live," exclaimed Red. "And all his merry band, by the look of it."

"Not so merry as they were when we saw them last," I said, a trifle pleased I must confess.

The prisoners were indeed in a pitiful condition. Fourneaux still held himself like a man, but the remainder had sunk to the ground in helpless heaps as soon as the guards let go of them. Through the gaps in their clothing it was possible, even from where we stood, to see the blood and filth caked on their skins. Some of them appeared to have wounds which, lacking treatment, had already begun to fester. Flies and other insects crawled on them so that one sickened at the sight. All except Fourneaux were bound and gagged with moss or tree bark.

"My God!" cried Laudonniere in a great shout that reached the fort easily, "if you have ill-treated my men you shall pay for this on your own body."

He had his hand on the hilt of his sword and the sword half drawn as he said this, and for a moment it seemed as if he would run the chief through there and then. But Saturiba did not flinch. He met Laudonniere's eyes without a flicker of his own, and the sword stayed half in, half out of the scabbard. The two men were like a piece of dramatic statuary, holding for ever in stone the moment but one before death. Death himself should have been one of the group, smiling softly and ready for anything.

At that point Pierre stepped between the two men and said quickly, "Fourneaux has betrayed you, sir. Saturiba brings him back to you that you may punish him with your own justice."

Slowly Laudonniere relaxed. We on the walls relaxed too, finding our fingers white and cramped on our weapons.

A sort of sigh passed over the whole fort as everyone breathed out and glanced thankfully aside at his neighbor. Half prepared as we were, we should have stood little chance against Saturiba's seven or eight hundred fighting men.

Laudonniere turned slowly away from the chief and towards the boy. Then, so quickly that few saw what happened, he struck Pierre a great blow on the side of the head with his open hand and tumbled him to the ground.

For a moment Saturiba's bodyguard quivered alert. Many of them had their throwing spears poised, on the point of hurling them at Laudonniere's body, but a small movement of the chief's hand prevented them. Had the blow landed on brown flesh instead of on white, those spears would have been whistling through the air before the sound of the blow reached the first trees of the forest. Instead there was merely a throaty exclamation from Saturiba himself which might have expressed approval, disapproval or even amusement. None of us could tell.

Pierre leapt immediately to his feet and out of Laudonniere's reach. "How have I deserved that?" he cried.

"For the underhand way in which you have crept into a position of importance," drawled Laudonniere in that slow, dandified voice he assumed when he was past the heat of anger. "Now tell me what it was you had to tell."

Pierre stood for a while silent, stiffly upright and terribly pale. He seemed, I thought, to be considering whether to speak or not. He wanted to strike back at Laudonniere and revenge his hurt. Then he seemed to put the thought from him and in a quiet respectful voice told his story. I was certain, however, that he had merely postponed his revenge till another day.

"The story, sir, goes like this," he said, "and I can vouch for much of it as I have been a witness.

"These men, with Fourneaux as their leader, are all that remains of a larger party that came ashore from the ships five days ago. They came through the forest to Saturiba's village where they demanded a guide to lead them here. Saturiba sent with them his youngest son, thinking to honor them, and the party, after feasting and passing the night in the village, went off into the forest.

"Saturiba's son led them to within a quarter of a mile of this place, and then they suddenly bound him with ropes and carried him off deeper into the forest. Somehow or other they had obtained information that another Indian chief named Potanou, an enemy of Saturiba, was rich in gold and precious jewels. Potanou's tribe live some distance inland, and Fourneaux and his party marched westward to find him.

"In two days they reached Potanou's camp, met the chief and offered to give him Saturiba's son in exchange for certain pieces of silver the chief wore on his clothing—"

"There was no gold, then?" interrupted Laudonniere.

"No, sir. No gold."

"Yes, yes. Go on, then," said Laudonniere.

"The exchange was made," went on Pierre. "Fourneaux received his silver and Potanou took Saturiba's son and and had him lashed up to a post set in the middle of the village. Whether this was a sort of pillory or whether they were preparing some ceremonial sacrifice, is not at all clear.

"Meanwhile Saturiba had become worried and sent out scouts to look for his son. They returned with the story of what had occurred and Saturiba set out immediately with a war party to attack Potanou. He collected men from many smaller tribes on the way. He also took me with him—perhaps as a hostage; I'm not sure."

"When we reached Potanou's village a great battle took place. Fourneaux and the rest of the party joined with Potanou and did great damage among Saturiba's men with their arquebuses. Eventually we stormed the village, rescued the boy and took Fourneaux and his party prisoner. Those that are not here of the original landing party were either killed in battle or have since died of their wounds on the march."

"I see," said Laudonniere thoughtfully. "And now, I suppose, Saturiba demands some sort of vengeance done on them. What if I refuse?"

Pierre shrugged his shoulders. "Saturiba would have killed them out of hand after the battle," he said, "but I persuaded him that Frenchmen should have French justice."

"And by bringing a whole army to watch this—justice in action," snapped Laudonniere, "he forces me to punish whether I want to or not. Where is the justice in that?"

"I don't think any threat is meant by bringing so many men," said Pierre. "They would have dispersed to their homes but that they were curious to learn about French justice."

Laudonniere looked slowly round, letting his glance slip from face to face of the men lining the fort wall; the worried, the eager, the frightened, the indifferent even. He looked at Saturiba, passive and waiting; at Fourneaux, frightened yet trying to appear defiant; at Pierre again.

"Well, why not?" he said at last. "I'll do it, and take my own line whatever it costs. Tell the chief that we will hold a trial of these men after the manner of the French tomorrow morning. We shall need some of his men as witnesses, no doubt, so he had better prepare them to appear."

4

And believe it or not the court was actually held next morning before the whole population of the fort and hundreds of wondering Indians. The procedure was a little amateurish, perhaps, but justice was done, and in the French fashion. Pierre Gambi was in his element interpreting for the Indians who were called as witnesses, and at the same time keeping up a running comment on the proceedings for the benefit of Saturiba, who was watching with immense interest.

Fourneaux and the others were eventually found guilty of disobeying orders, of offending our friends and allies (meaning Saturiba) and of putting the whole settlement in danger. They were sentenced to be bastinadoed—this punishment being carried out on the spot—and returned to France by the next ship. Fourneaux, as the leader was given the additional punishment of having his right ear cut off. He was forbidden to carry arms for the next five years.

The Indians appeared to be much impressed, and Saturiba declared himself satisfied. Indeed it was interesting to watch these simple but savage folk receiving their first education in the civilized ways of the white man. They must have found much food for thought in the contrast between this court of law, rough and ready though it had been, and their own ignorant and barbarous manner of settling such problems.

Before the Indians withdrew from the fort, Laudonniere took the opportunity of showing Saturiba the strength of the walls and the action of our cannon. The demonstration of firing these weapons nearly caused a panic among the Indian army, many of them running away into the forest and not reappearing for some hours. Laudonniere's intention was to impress the Indians with our strength, and in this he certainly succeeded. But there was another side to this awe our weapons inspired in them which was to bear fruit later.

After the inspection of the fort Laudonniere and Saturiba held a private conference in the hut the Indians had built on the river bank. Pierre Gambi acted as interpreter, of course, and told Red and me in private what had taken place there.

It appeared that Saturiba had made a bargain. He offered to supply the fort with maize, meat and tobacco for a period of twelve months if Laudonniere would agree to assist him in his wars against the two rival Indian chiefs of the area, Potanou of whom we had already heard, and Outina whose people lived somewhat to the south.

"And he agreed?" asked Red.

"Of course he agreed," said Pierre. "What else would you expect? It was a fair bargain."

"I wonder?" said Red thoughtfully. "What shall we gain by mixing ourselves up with perpetual Indian wars?"

"Gold!" said Gambi with a laugh. "You know the old trick? Play one tribe off against the other."

"Gold!" exclaimed Red contemptuously. "I tell you

what; there's gold right here where I'm standing if we would only work for it."

Pierre stared at the earth under his feet with surprise. "Here?" he said. "How do you know?"

"Good fertile soil," said Red. "A year's hard work on this place and we should have a paradise. If we used half the energy wasted seeking gold on digging and planting the earth...."

"Oh, digging!" said Pierre distastefully, and turned rudely away.

Chapter Four

FARMING

IT was not very long before Red's gloomiest fears proved to be true. No sooner was the fort completed than the colonists were tumbling over themselves to get out of it and search for gold. Saturiba's promise of food supplies for a year was completely misunderstood. The Indians had supposed that the new white colonists had come to till the land, and being good farmers themselves they knew that the land gives no return for the first year. The promise of food was to carry the whites over until their own crops began to ripen.

The colonists, however, like the grasshopper in the fable, seemed to think that because the Indians were feeding them they had no need to work for themselves, but could devote the whole of their time trying to find the gold and precious stones they had heard so much about.

To make matters worse a young trader named La Roche Ferriere, who had come with the colonists but since gone off on his own among the more distant Indian tribes to trade and explore, had sent back a messenger to Laudonniere with exaggerated stories of the riches to be found in the Appalachian Mountains some distance into the interior of the country. With the message came presents: a mantle of woven feathers, arrows with points of gold, quivers made from rare furs and decorated with precious stones and large wedge-shaped pieces of some green stone that many vowed to be emerald although none had ever seen emeralds of such a size before.

For a couple of days the colonists were in a ferment about these gifts. The gold-tipped arrows, they said, proved that Ferriere had reached some place where gold was the common metal and was used as we use iron. Laudonniere was of the opinion that these arrows had been the property of some Indian chief, were purchased or even stolen by Ferriere and were merely of ceremonial importance and proved nothing. But no one listened to Laudonniere. Finally he bowed to the storm and sent one of the nobles, a middle-aged and reliable man named Grotaut, to follow Ferriere and discover how much truth there was in the story.

For a week this satisfied the colonists, but when nothing was heard from Grotaut they began to demand that Laudonniere give general permission to explore. Laudonniere refused, saying that if all the colonists went off it would leave the fort too vulnerable to enemy attack.

He had very little command over them, however, and that night some fifty of the colonists slipped quietly out of the fort. Among them went Pierre Gambi.

Pierre told us of his intentions before he went, and swore us to secrecy. Red tried to persuade him of the danger and stupidity of what he was going to do, but Pierre would not listen.

"You go and dig your moldy old earth," he said, "and stay here for the rest of your life, if you want to. I'm going to get rich as quickly as I can."

"What's the use of being rich here?" asked Red. "You cannot spend the gold when you have it."

"Here?" exclaimed Pierre. "Who's going to stay in this hole? I tell you, I shall be richer than a cardinal in a year or two. Then I shall return to France and become a great man."

2

With the departure of so many of the colonists the fort became a very quiet place. Laudonniere sent one of the ships back to France about this time and in it went a dozen of the malcontents who had followed Fourneaux into the forest on that first landing. The only people left in the fort were the soldiers and their officers and a few craftsmen like old Chabrier, the carpenter. Le Moyne the artist stayed of course, and there were in addition half a dozen colonists who had no desire to explore.

I remained to serve Laudonniere and very lonely work it was, too. The man was ill again, spending much of his time in his house either walking restlessly up and down, his fingers fidgeting in his beard, or lying absolutely motionless on his bed. His eyes, hollowed with sickness, stared all the time out through the timbers of the walls. I asked him once what he was looking at.

He stopped suddenly in his pacing up and down and with a tremendous effort focused his eyes on my face. "I am looking at the past," he said, "and it frightens me."

"You mean the future, don't you?" I said.

He shook his head violently. "The past!" he insisted. "I . . . listen, boy . . ." He put his hand on my arm and stared at me so intently that I thought he meant I was to listen to some sound outside in the fort.

"It is only old Chabrier sawing wood," I said.

He waved the interruption aside. "You have heard," he said, "of the expedition that sailed to these parts under Jean Ribaut . . ."

"Of course," I said. "It failed. They all came back."

"Not all," said Laudonniere quickly. "No, not all."

I remembered hearing that some of the returning colonists from that party had been picked up by English sailors and imprisoned in England and thought perhaps he was thinking of those.

"I was with Jean Ribaut," said Laudonniere slowly. Then he paused for a long time, still holding my arm, and I thought perhaps he had forgotten what he was talking about. Then suddenly he withdrew his hand and turned away. "But not now," he muttered to himself. "Not now."

Later I told Red about this, and he was of the opinion that Laudonniere had some crime on his conscience; a crime connected in some way with the earlier expedition.

"I expect he needs to tell someone about it," he added. "They say that confession is good for the soul."

"Well," I said, "he's tried twice now, and failed."

"Third time lucky," said Red with a laugh. "But look,

I've got something to tell you; can you listen to me instead."

"A confession?" I said.

"Not exactly. It's simply that ... well, I've been talking to a few of the colonists, and half a dozen of them seem to be of my opinion. . . ."

"About getting down to some work on the land?" I said.

"Yes, just that. Nothing's been done about it. There were agricultural implements brought in the ships, but as far as we can make out they're still there. Everybody's been ready enough to exchange some worthless piece of glass for a wedge of silver or a gold earring, but as for unloading a few hoes or a plough ... well, as I say. . . ."

Red was beginning to work himself up into his usual state of indignation about the way the colony was being run. I tried to bring him back to his subject by asking what he intended to do about it.

"That's the point," he answered. "These other settlers have agreed with me that we ought to do something. It's no good waiting for Laudonniere to tell us; we must go and ask permission to leave the fort and set up farms."

"Why do you ask me?" I said. "I haven't any magic powers over Laudonniere."

"For two reasons," said Red. "In the first place I'd like to have you along with me. It'll be lonely work and hard work, and I'd sooner share it with a friend."

"Thank you for that," I said. "And the other reason?"

"You have the ear of the chief," he said. "You serve him and see him daily."

"You want me to ask for you, is that it?" I said.

"Nothing of the sort," he exclaimed roughly, hurt perhaps at my manner. "We could ask him for ourselves when we met him about the fort. But he is no longer to be seen. He keeps to his dwelling for days together...."

"He is very ill again," I said.

"No doubt. And I'm sorry to hear it. But the point is we cannot see him to ask unless he will receive us. I'd hoped you might approach him on the matter."

"I'll see what I can do ... gladly," I said, and left him.

There was no doubt that Red had been deeply hurt by my manner, but I could not pretend to be enthusiastic for his idea. It did not attract me in the least. I know nothing of working on the land and have always looked on the typical farm laborer as an uncouth sort of fellow. At the same time I was more than half convinced that Pierre Gambi was right and Red was wrong. From the little I'd seen of the American continent it did not strike me as the sort of place I should wish to spend the rest of my life in. I had been reared in a print shop, never far from the smell of ink and the sound of clicking type and rumbling presses. I could enjoy the silent forests and strange Indians as if it were an extravagant holiday, but they would not do, I felt, as permanent companions.

I know now that Red was right and Pierre was wrong, but there is little virtue in being wiser after the event. At the time, as I say, I was more inclined towards the idea of gold-seeking, but lacked the courage to set off on my own.

However, I kept my word and told Laudonniere that there were certain of the settlers concerned about getting the implements out of the ships and commencing work on the land.

"Rare birds," he commented, and told me to bring

them to him at once. Within an hour I had brought Red and two others to him to explain what they wanted.

"Where would you think of setting up these farms?" he asked, after he had heard what they had to say.

"Farther towards the river mouth," answered Red promptly. "There is much fertile land on the north bank there, which we noticed on our first trip upriver."

"That is where the main Indian farms lie, isn't it?" said Laudonniere. "If you take cultivated land from the natives it will lead to trouble for the whole colony."

"The thought had never occurred to us," said Red indignantly. "We should go beyond their land to those plains that lie farther from the river."

"So far away?" said Laudonniere thoughtfully. "We should not be able to protect you there, you know. The Indians would be between you and the fort. They could do you what hurt they liked, and we could do nothing."

"Why should they wish to hurt us?" asked Red. "We should be neighbors, and good ones I hope."

Laudonniere shrugged his shoulders. He seemed to have lost interest. "Be it on your own heads then," he said. "I'll give you a note to the ships. You may draw what stores you need tomorrow—"

"Or today?" said Red.

Laudonniere smiled. "I thought farmers were supposed to be slow and cautious," he commented. "Yes, very well, today if you wish it. And there is only one condition; for the first five years of your farming adventure you must hand over to the fort one tenth of your crops. This is a payment for the implements, and for what little protection our presence here will be to you."

He sat down to scribble a note that would give Red

the authority to draw his material from the ships' stores. As he waited for the ink to dry he turned to me. "I suppose you will be wanting to go and keep your friend company?" he said.

I hesitated, in very real doubt. If I refused to go with Red, he would be so hurt that I should probably lose my only friend; if I said I wanted to go Laudonniere might be angry at my deserting him. And behind all that I was not at all sure what I did want to do; farming was not my sort of work and I doubted whether I had the sort of strength and endurance necessary for it, and at the same time I was heartily sick of playing nurse to Laudonniere.

"Well?" insisted Laudonniere, "which do you want; to stay or to go?"

I still kept an embarrassed silence, glancing quickly at my friend, at Laudonniere, and then keeping my eyes down for safety on the floor. Laudonniere only half understood my difficulty.

"Come," he said with a laugh, "I see what it is. You do not want to hurt my feelings by showing your eagerness to go. That is it, confess now!"

I mumbled something.

"This is what you must do then," he said, leaning forward and catching hold of my arm in the friendliest gesture I'd known him to make. "Go with your friend and give him all the help you can. One alone against the rich wilderness is not enough. Learn all you can and get healthy and strong, and at the end of six months come back to me and let me see you again."

I thanked him as convincingly as I could. Red was obviously delighted and I tried to appear so.

3

A week later Red and I stood, with our gear heaped around us, on the spot Red had chosen for his farm. With a whole continent to chose from one can afford to be particular and Red had taken three days picking out his land. We had dragged our way for miles across grassy plains, cut our way through forests and waded thigh deep in mud through marshes before Red had been finally satisfied. He had taken me visiting the Indian farms to see the soil, the method of cultivation, the sort of crops and implements, and he talked farming for hours and days on end until I was ready to scream. My head was buzzing with expressions I had never heard before and only partly understood, and my feet were so weary and sore that it was a torture to walk. Red seemed not to notice my condition. He was so obsessed with his ideas that he had no time for anything but the quality of soil, the drainage, and the best crops of the neighboring farms.

And when we had finally settled on the best place, there still remained all the tools and gear to carry from the ships. We had the help of half a dozen sailors for the first day, during which time we shifted the gear up the river and stacked it on the river bank. But the farm was nearly two miles from the main river, up a narrow creek too shallow for the ships' boats, and from that point we had to do the carrying by ourselves. The smaller tools went in an Indian canoe we bought, but the heavier implements had to be taken to pieces and carried. When the last piece was fetched I felt I could have sunk to the ground and slept for a month.

Red lifted the heavy wooden colter off his shoulder and set it gently on the ground. "Ah," he said, stretching his back and looking round, "now, we can really make a start."

I groaned from utter weariness and Red laughed.

"All right, Pierre," he said, "you have earned a little rest. Have a sleep now—your strength will soon return. When you wake you can get a fire going and we'll have a good, hot meal. I'll just tidy up a little."

He seized an ax from the pile of tools and strode off in the direction of the forest.

I lay on the ground for a few minutes longer, feeling as if all my bones and muscles had turned to water. I must not let him patronize me, I thought to myself. As long as he is working I must work. I must drive myself . . .

The sun beat down on the long grass and I shut my eyes against the glare. It was about midday. I thought I would count a hundred slowly to myself and then get up and start work again. Sweat began to trickle through my hair like the movement of insects. I began to count.

When I opened my eyes again, the sun was on the point of setting and a cool fresh breeze was blowing up from the river and bending the tops of the tall grasses. I had a dry, burnt taste in my mouth and my head ached abominably. I sat up stiffly and looked around. There was no sign of Red but from some distance came the rhythmical sound of hammering.

I got stiffly to my feet and looked in the direction of the sound. Red was banging a post into the ground about a quarter of a mile away. He saw me and waved and then went on with his banging.

I must pull myself together, I told myself. Fire, yes, light a fire. That's right.

Everything near at hand seemed to have changed. The grass had been cut in a wide circle around me, the gear had been stacked up neatly and covered over with sackcloth, and a huge pile of brushwood had made its appearance. Just near me was a large earthenware pitcher filled to the brim with cold water, and next to it lay the bodies of three brightly colored birds arranged in a row on the grass. Red had been very busy, it seemed.

When I had sluiced my face and taken a few mouthfuls of water from the pitcher, I began to feel better. I set about lighting a fire and preparing the birds. This at least, I thought, was a task I could manage.

Red had chosen his farm on the edge of the wide grassy plain to the north of the river. On three sides the view was open for miles with only the faintest blue streak of a mountain range in the west. South of us, and between us and the river, was the forest. The Indians said that the storm winds came from the south, the rain winds from the east, and the dry winds from the north and west, and Red had sited his farm accordingly so that the forest would break the force of the crop-destroying winds. On the other hand, we were far enough away from the trees to be safe from the forest insect and animal life. The Indians said that out on the plains one only had to worry about wandering herds of deer which might, in one night, eat all one's crops.

Red came back just after the sun had gone down.

"Well?" he said, rubbing his hands before the fire and looking at me with a grin, "and how do you feel?"

"I didn't mean to go to sleep," I said.

"Nonsense," he said. "Just what you needed."

"But you didn't sleep," I said.

Red laughed, "Me?" he said. "I happened to be born with the body of an ox. It's no credit to me. But I don't know how you've managed to keep going."

"These birds are just about cooked," I said, taking them away from the fire. I felt embarrassed by his praise, but pleased with myself that I'd not disappointed him.

We ate in silence for a while, and then Red leaned back with a sigh and gathered up a handful of the dried grass. "You know," he said, wiping his greasy fingers and throwing the grass on the fire, "I've got it all planned out."

"The farm?" I said.

"No, not the farm. I've had that planned for months. I meant our behavior towards the Indians."

I laughed. "What Indians?" I said. "I haven't seen a soul all day."

"They're not far off, though," Red said. "And we shall be seeing them from time to time. We shall need to do a little trading with them. We need seed, for a start...."

"We brought sacks of seed off the boat—" I began.

"French seed," said Red. "How do we know it'll be any use here? I'll give it a try, of course, but I don't want to rely on that. I'd like to experiment with this Indian corn—maize they call it, don't they? But anyway, it's not just that. It's the whole question of how to treat these Indian chaps. You know, they've done it all wrong up at the fort. We shall have to make an entirely new start if we want to survive out here by ourselves."

"Well?" I said.

"The Indians thought the first white men were gods,"

said Red. "They treated them with respect. But now they're beginning to realize their mistake. They'll go to the opposite extreme and think we're fools and knaves next. Then they'll realize that the whites can't exist without the Indians' help... and when they realize that, God help the fort."

"What can we do?" I said.

"We shall have to start all over again with them," said Red. "We must treat them as our equals and we must be quick to learn their language and their ways. And now and then we must be able to do something better than they can do it, so that they will want to learn from us too. In that way we shall make friends. Well," he added abruptly, "bedtime, I think. We want to be fresh for a good day's work tomorrow."

"And tomorrow," I said as I got into my blankets, "we begin work on the cabin, eh?"

"Cabin?" exclaimed Red. "We can't afford to waste a day on building a cabin. Tomorrow we start ploughing. And there's not a day to lose."

I had just begun to wonder where Red was going to find the oxen to pull the plough when I fell asleep.

4

And yet I might have guessed the answer to that: there were no oxen; we pulled the plough ourselves. For the next day and the day after that, and the day after that and for many weary days, we fought with the soil that Red had chosen for a farm. We cut the long grass and when the sun had dried it we raked it up and built three large hayricks. Then we set fire to the stubble and roots.

We had to do this with great care, only burning a small patch at a time in case the flames got out of hand. Red made two long flails of old sailcloth which we soaked in the stream near at hand and used to control the flames.

During the time we were burning the ground we had to take it in turns to sleep, for the grass roots smoldered for hours and were a constant danger; a light puff of wind—and the wind seemed to rise at nighttime and disappear with the sun—was enough to bring up spurts of flame from all over the ground that we thought had burned dead.

When one small patch of ground was cleared in this way we ploughed it. Slow and painful work this was, with one of us in the traces to pull and the other at the shafts to guide the plough. We had not the strength to make a deep clean furrow, but merely broke up the cindered grass roots and scratched at the surface of the soil. It would do for the first year, Red thought, as the ground was so rich.

The strangest sight was the sudden arrival of the birds. Before we had finished our first furrow Red cried out, "Here comes help."

I looked up quickly expecting to see that some people from the fort had come out, but the plain was empty.

"In the sky," said Red, pointing.

A large flock of birds was circling doubtfully round us, screaming and shrieking and gradually coming lower. In a few minutes they had begun to settle on the turned ground behind us, and within an hour they were diving to our very feet for the grubs and worms turned up by our plough.

"At least we know where to get today's dinner from,"

I said cheerfully. Some of the birds were large wading birds from the banks of the river and one of them would have made a good meal for the two of us.

But Red was almost angry with me for this. "We'll shoot those when we're starving, and not before," he exclaimed. And when he was calmer he explained to me how the birds were cleaning the soil of insect pests that would spoil the crops later. I still had a lot to learn.

5

At the end of the month we had ploughed and sown the original area Red had marked out with his posts. It was as much, he thought, as we should be able to handle for the first season. He planned, of course, to go on adding more and more land each year.

"And now," he said, "we'll build ourselves a first-rate cabin and make ourselves comfortable."

I jumped to my feet and picked up the large felling ax and Red burst out laughing. "We must let our dinner digest first," he said. "There's no hurry."

"I've been looking forward to building the cabin," I said.

Red got slowly to his feet and putting one long arm round my shoulders gave me a hug that made my bones crack. "I've never known such a change in anyone," he said. "Do you remember that day when you lay on your back in the sun and tried to count a hundred before you started to make the fire?"

I nodded. "It's the fresh air and the hard work," I confessed. "I'll never go back into a print shop again as long as I live."

We stared at each other solemnly, like a couple of owls, for a few moments and then Red broke away with a short laugh and picked up the bow saw. As we walked towards the forest he said awkwardly, "I've a sort of confession to make; you must promise not to be hurt."

I promised.

"Do you remember when I was seeing Laudonniere about getting the gear from the ships? Well, he turned and asked you if you wanted to come along with me, but he didn't ask me if I wanted you. . . ."

"You mean, you didn't want me?" I exclaimed.

Red stared straight ahead towards the forest and gave a quick, embarrassed nod. "I thought you would be a drag on me and prevent me getting things done," he added. "Oh, I can say that now because things have turned out so very different. But you will forgive me for . . . well, for not being very pleased with Laudonniere?"

Now it was my turn to laugh. "To be fair, I must confess, too," I said. "I didn't want to come, but I didn't dare say so for fear of hurting your feelings."

Red let out a great roar, dropped his bow saw on the ground and charged at me. The next moment we were rolling on the ground, rubbing each other's face in the dirt like a couple of schoolboys. It ended as it was bound to end; with me lying spreadeagled on my back, Red sitting astride my chest with his great knees bruising my arm muscles. "Say you give in," he said.

"I give in," I said quickly.

"Tell you what," he said as we walked on, "when we've finished this cabin, let's take a couple of days off. Let's go down to the fort and see how they all are."

"Good idea," I said. "And they might have had word from Pierre. I wonder if he has found any gold."

"If anyone has found gold, Pierre has," said Red.

But as it turned out we didn't have to go to the fort for news, for on the day we finished the cabin we had our first visitor. We were working round the outside wedging a mixture of clay and dried grass into the cracks between the logs of the walls when we heard a great hail from the direction of the forest and turned to see Sergeant La Caille striding across the plain towards us.

He seemed pleased to see us, and we were certainly pleased to see him. "So this is where you've been hiding yourselves," he boomed out when he was still a hundred yards away.

"How did you find us?" asked Red when La Caille had come near enough.

"Devil of a job," said La Caille. "Very devil of a job. Laudonniere said, 'Go out and see if those farmers are all right.' You know what he is. 'Where shall I find them?' I said. He flared up, you know his way. 'How should I know where they are?' he shouted at me. 'Go and find them and report back in two days.' So here I am."

"Well, you did find us," grinned Red. "And you're just in time to eat with us. We've got a nice haunch of venison that has been waiting for someone with a big appetite."

The sergeant licked his lips. "Venison, eh? And us living on parched corn and stale fish. You certainly knew what you were up to when you came out here."

La Caille came round the farm with us and praised all he saw and then sat down and stuffed himself with venison until he could hardly move. He looked thinner and older than when we had seen him last, and he wore a continual look of worry. Red mentioned this to him and he grinned and wiped his hand across his forehead as if to clear the wrinkles away.

"Worried?" he said. "So would you be. Devil of a mess we're in back there. You've missed it all. Indian war. Politics. Treachery. And all for nothing. Saturiba's against us now. And the other two as well. Can't remember their silly names."

"Outina and Potanou?" I said.

"That's it," said La Caille. "Those. They all hate us. We can't leave the fort nowadays except in parties of six or more. Laudonniere's orders. Soldiers being mysteriously killed. Men vanished into thin air. Devil of a mess."

Gradually, as he sat digesting his meal, Red and I managed to get from La Caille a general outline of what had been happening at the fort during the last month. He told the story in his own peculiar way, spitting out the fragments of sentences like broken teeth, leaving much to the imagination.

It appeared that Saturiba had asked for help against Outina, reminding Laudonniere of his bargain. Twenty men had been sent and the effect of their arquebuses—the magic weapons of which all the Indians were frightened—had been to make the affair an overwhelming victory for Saturiba. Hundreds of Outina's tribe had been massacred and some dozen or so prisoners taken for a ceremonial sacrifice.

At this point Laudonniere had received information that there was gold to be found in mountains beyond Outina's country.

"About face," said La Caille. "Like some silly children's game; everybody change sides. You see, we needed to be friends with Outina so's to get our hands on his gold. But Outina didn't want to be friends with us after the way our soldiers had been shooting up his people. Naturally."

"So?" said Red.

"So Laudonniere has a brilliant idea. He sends to Saturiba and asks for two of the prisoners as a reward for our part in the battle. After a while Saturiba gives in. Two prisoners. Then Laudonniere sends them back to Outina with his compliments."

"Well, that was clever," I said. "You must admit—"

"But not clever enough," said La Caille. "Why? Because Saturiba's in a rage because we returned his prisoners, and Outina's not impressed with receiving two when he's had a hundred or more murdered with arquebus fire."

"So the fort is out of favor with the Indians," said Red thoughtfully. "That is the worst thing that could happen."

"We'll manage," said La Caille. "I've been in worse straits. Why, this is nothing compared with the first time we came here. Laudonniere was second in command then, you know. Under Jean Ribaut. Now there's a man...."

"I've had a feeling," I said, "that something happened on that earlier voyage. Something horrible. Laudonniere's been on the point of telling me about it twice, but each time he stopped himself. Whatever it was I think that is what causes him to have these fits of illness and depression."

La Caille looked at me shrewdly for a few moments, and there was something in his expression that I could not fathom. "Yes," he said, drawing the word out. "Well, I'd better be getting back. Make my report. Say you're doing well and send your regards, eh?"

"We've got a few haunches of venison we've been trying to smoke-cure," said Red. "Would you take one back as a present to Laudonniere?"

"Well, now, I don't think that would be wise," said La Caille. "You see, we're on short rations back at the fort, and if it got around that you had food here to spare...."

"I see what you mean," said Red. "It was kind of you to think of us."

We walked back to the river with Sergeant La Caille. He had a boat waiting for him there. On the way I tried once or twice to steer him back to talk about the voyage under Ribaut, but he refused to say anything about it.

Finally, as he pushed off from the bank, he cried out to us, "Is there anything I can do for you back at the fort? Any message you'd like passed on? Anything?"

"I don't think so," said Red.

"Is there any news of Gambi?" I asked.

La Caille smacked his thigh with annoyance. "There now," he exclaimed. "I knew there was something I had to tell you. The young rascal's been back two or three times since you left. He brought down some loads of alligator skins to be sent back to France when the ship sails—"

"Wait a moment," cried Red. "What ship? You haven't told us half the news."

"You wouldn't be interested in that," said La Caille

scornfully. "Rats leaving the sinking ship! Some of them sick of it and going back to France. No. But this Gambi lad, he's done well for himself. Married the daughter of an Indian chief on some island or other. Can't remember the name. Making himself rich, he is."

"Married!" I exclaimed. "Pierre Gambi married!"

"So he says. But you must come up to the fort in a month's time and see him. He said he'd be coming again before the ship sailed."

La Caille nodded to the sailors to hoist sail and then as the boat dipped and got under way he waved cheerfully at us. "That's it," he cried. "Come up and see us. Take a day off!"

6

But a month later we were so busy that we couldn't find the time to go on a visit to the fort—not even to see Pierre Gambi—so we put it off.

In fact we were busy training the two eagles we had been given some months earlier by the old Indian chief. Up till now we had no time to spare for them. We had kept their wings bound with leather thongs in the Indian way and allowed them to wander about the farm at will. For the most part we simply ignored them. And this, contrary to the usual way of training birds to hawking, had done half our training for us. The creatures had become used to us and as tame as barnyard fowls. They took us for granted. Sometimes we would not see them for a whole day, but they always returned at night to roost on a rough perch in the cabin. At the same time they were unable to find much meat for themselves, so they came to us to be fed—usually at meal times—and took pieces of raw flesh from our fingers.

By this time they were almost full grown. They had had their first molt and were beginning to look magnificent in their glossy adult plumage.

One day Red went to the gunpowder keg and found it almost empty. "We shall have to go to the fort soon," he said, "to get some more powder. We use far too much. We ought to think of some ways of trapping and snaring our dinner meat."

"We could use the bow more often," I said, trying to think of the usual ways of killing game. "Or we could get hold of a hawk somehow."

"A hawk!" exclaimed Red. "Aren't we fools?"

"I don't see—" I began, a little on my dignity.

"The eagles!" exclaimed Red. "They'd be magnificent."

At any other time the idea would have frightened me. The eagle is a large and exceeding fierce bird to handle on the fist. He is seldom flown at game, and even less often successfully. But these two birds of ours had become so used to us that we had almost ceased to regard them as eagles.

So we tried it. It was no use hooding them in the usual way for they had grown used to their freedom. It was well known, however, that the Saracens and Turks flew their hawks without hoods; we could but try.

The strangest thing was that we had to teach them to fly. They had been walking for so long with their wings bound that it did not seem to occur to them to rise in the air. They went about for the first couple of days after we had cut the thongs with their wings held uncomfortably half-spread, rather like angry swans.

In the end I had the idea of throwing one of them out of a tree. We took them down to the edge of the forest and there, with an eagle protesting on my shoulder, I set about climbing a large maple tree. The bird scored me badly with his talons, being frightened no doubt, but I bore it as best I could and went on up until I was about forty feet from the ground. There I sat in a fork with my legs twined around the trunk for safety and transferred the eagle to my wrist. Red, standing below and some distance out on the plain, then showed a great piece of raw meat in his hand and tried to call the bird down to him.

But the eagle would not budge. He saw the meat and showed eagerness to get at it, but he would not fly. Red tossed the meat into the air and called again, but the eagle only moved nervously on my wrist, changing his grip and punching holes in my flesh. My hand was becoming numb because of the strength of the eagle's grip.

I transferred him to a level branch with the idea of climbing down and leaving him there, but he seemed to sense my intention for he quickly tried to scramble back on my shoulder, flapping his wings wildly and knocking me silly with the force of them. I clutched desperately at a branch, missed and fell to the next. I had the satisfaction of seeing the eagle, dislodged from my shoulder, flutter desperately down to the ground. It landed clumsily a few yards from Red's feet, ruffled itself angrily and then proceeded to look about for the piece of meat it knew to be lying somewhere in the grass.

"Are you all right?" called Red.

I had caught the next branch down, and after swinging in mid-air for a few seconds with the sick taste of fear in my mouth, I had managed to scramble back into a safer position in the tree.

"It gave me a scare," I said. "I'm all right, though. And the creature did fly, didn't it?"

As I said this I turned to get a more secure grip in my new position and happened to glance into the next tree. A man was squatting in a crotch, looking anxiously at me. His face was familiar; a face I remembered seeing about the fort. A man called Gièvre.

He put his fingers to his lips to indicate silence and then pointed down at the ground as if there was something there he feared. I could see nothing, except Red and the two eagles. I thought the man must have gone mad.

By the time I had climbed down the tree again Red had run some distance out on to the plain, trying to get the eagles to fly to the lure. One of them was doing so—the one that had been pitched out of the tree—but the other was hopping over the ground like a great clumsy crow. I looked up into the tree but could see no sign of Gièvre. It was all very puzzling.

Then as I stood there, still wondering what the man could be doing, what he could have meant by his strange signs, two soldiers from the fort came out of the forest about a hundred yards farther along and stood for a moment to get their bearings. When they saw me they turned and came along towards me. They looked dissatisfied and bored. One of them I knew slightly; he went by the nickname of the Grocer, on account of the ingratiating way he had of rubbing his hands together. It was he who spoke first.

"Thought we might find you here somewhere," he

said, not troubling to greet me or show surprise at seeing me. "They said you were out here with that red-headed fellow. Farming or something."

"That's right," I said. I had no liking for the man and made no attempt to be friendly.

"Do you know a chap called Gièvre?" he asked.

"Gièvre? A soldier?"

"No," he spat the word out, "a nobleman. Pasty-faced, with a square nose stuck in the middle . . . like a sundial."

"I think I know the man you mean," I said.

"We're looking for him," said the Grocer.

I pretended to look interested but said nothing. So the man up the tree wasn't mad at any rate.

"Got to take him back," said the Grocer.

"Why?" I asked. "What's he done?"

"How should I know?" He shrugged his shoulders contemptuously. "Orders. Bring him back, they said. What a hope!" He swept his arm vaguely round to indicate the whole continent.

"A difficult task," I agreed politely.

The two soldiers stared at me for a few moments, and then the Grocer muttered something and they turned back towards the forest. As they entered the shade of the trees the Grocer looked back at me. "If you lay eyes on him," he said, "you'd better get a message up to the fort."

"Yes," I said.

I stood where I was until the two soldiers were out of sight and then hurried across to Red to tell him of Gièvre in the tree and the search that was being made for him. We went back together to the place where I had seen him.

"You'd better come down now," called Red up the tree. Nothing happened.

"Gièvre! The soldiers have gone!"

Gièvre's pallid face showed round the trunk of the tree staring down at us solemnly. Then he nodded and began to climb down.

7

That evening in our cabin Gièvre had a queer story to tell us. As we discovered later he did not tell the whole truth but colored his story so that it favored him. We discovered the rest of the facts later so I shall tell it here in its more complete form.

It appeared that almost immediately after Red and I had left the fort the dissatisfaction with Laudonniere had become more acute. The main reason for it was Laudonniere's ruling that no settlers should go off by themselves trading with the Indians and looking for gold. Some who had gone earlier had lately returned and none of them had been successful. The trading stores were getting low.

Laudonniere then ruled that private individuals should no longed be allowed to use the trading stores, and that in future all attempts to find gold in the province must originate from him. The result of this was a growing feeling of dissatisfaction.

Then one of the ships was to return to France in an attempt to hasten the relief ships which were now long overdue. Now that all the Indians had been antagonized there was the possibility that the fort might be starved out if Saturiba stopped his supplies of food.

At this point our man Gièvre, with the knowledge of half a dozen rebels in the fort, had written a long letter to Admiral Coligny accusing Laudonniere of favoritism, injustice, chicanery, embezzlement and many more crimes. He had given the letter to a young nobleman named Marillac who was to return in the ship.

This Marillac was a coxcomb and a bit of a fool and he had tried to sell the letter to Laudonniere. Laudonniere had refused to trade and dismissed the young nobleman contemptuously, but afterwards he had called Gièvre to his quarters and warned him of the dangers of getting himself mixed up with the malcontents. Gièvre had misunderstood the warning and had fled from the fort.

"Well," said Red when Gièvre's rigmarole was finished, "one thing's clear out of all that; there's a mutiny brewing at the fort."

"Laudonniere has few friends," said Gièvre. "Fourneaux will take over."

"Fourneaux is a mealymouthed rogue," said Red.

"Anyway," I said, "Laudonniere has control of the army. What chance has a mutiny of success?"

"The soldiers follow their officers," said Gièvre, "and most of the officers are with Fourneaux."

"We are lucky to be out of it all," I said thankfully.

Red looked at me with raised eyebrows. "Out of it?" he said. "How can we be out of it? We're going straight back to the fort tomorrow morning to offer our assistance to Laudonniere."

The expression on his face prevented me from arguing about it.

Chapter Five

MUTINY

So back we went to the fort early next morning well loaded with meat from our private store and with our weapons concealed in our blanket rolls. I for one felt the folly of it. We had been safe from disturbance at the farm, there was plenty of work to be done and the doing of it more useful than playing rebels in the suspicion-ridden atmosphere of the fort. Red did not attempt to convince me; he simply assumed it was the natural thing to do; I was carried along with him like a floating leaf in the wake of a moving boat.

We left Gièvre at the cabin with the promise that we would not betray him. Not that we sympathized with the man in any way; he was our guest. We left one of the eagles with instructions for its feeding, but took the other with us.

We arrived in the fort in the middle of the morning and the first person we saw was Pierre Gambi, loading his canoe on the strand.

He came towards us with outstretched arms, in his usual demonstrative way. He was as full of himself as ever, bubbling over with the story of his own success and giving us no time to answer his questions or tell him of our own little venture.

"How well you look," he cried. "I can't tell you how good it is to see a friendly face again. They're all as glum as toadstools in the fort. Even Arlac is a dull dog nowadays. Come with me to my island. The two of you. We'll all get rich together. I've struck gold, my friends. Not the sort of gold I was looking for, but gold nevertheless."

He put one finger to the side of his nose and looked at us with his head slyly on one side. "A thousand alligator skins," he whispered. "Just think of it! I shall go back to France with them in a few months' time. Laudonniere has promised me. And then you'll see. Before I've finished I'll buy Le Havre. I'll be mayor with a gold chain round my neck—"

"Wait, wait," said Red laughing. "You have me out of breath already. A thousand alligator skins, did you say?"

"Well, I haven't got a thousand yet," Pierre admitted. "But it won't be long. I have a little scheme that I'm going to try out when I get back to Edelano."

"We heard you'd married an Indian princess," I said.

"An exaggerated version of the truth," grinned Pierre.

"But there is truth in it?"

"Oh, yes," he said. "Timicane, she's called. The only daughter of the chief of Edelano. A nice girl, simple, ignorant, superstitious, and not too clean in her personal habits, but a nice girl all the same. And a wonderful cook."

He began to strut up and down a little in front of us; he never could stand still while he talked.

"And you think Le Havre will be pleased to have a mayor with a brown-skinned wife?" I said.

Pierre Gambi stopped his strutting and turned to me with an expression of exaggerated horror. "But my dear friend," he said, laying one hand on my arm, "you don't suppose I shall take her back to France with me, do you?"

"You're married to her," said Red bluntly.

"I had to marry her to get my present position," said Pierre. "It was a political marriage, nothing more. And in any case as a good Christian I cannot consider myself bound by a heathen wedding ceremony."

"I don't see what that has to do with it," said Red.

Pierre looked from Red to me and then back, peering into our faces like some intelligent monkey considering which of his tricks will fetch him applause. "I think," he said at last, "I must tell you the whole story."

"I don't think I want to hear it," said Red stubbornly. "If the only way to get rich is by betraying simple people, then I would sooner remain poor."

"Betraying!" exclaimed Pierre. "How you talk!"

"Anyway," said Red, "we are off to report to Laudonniere and offer him our assistance."

"He's in need of it," grinned Pierre. "I feel quite sorry for him."

Red and I moved up the beach toward the fort but Pierre continued to stand by his canoe.

"Where will you be when we've finished?" asked Red.

"On my way up the river," replied Pierre a little sullenly.

"But . . . you will stay until we have settled this Fourneaux business?"

"Fourneaux will settle your business, more like," said Pierre. "You don't know the strength of feeling there yet. There are hardly half a dozen people to stand by Laudonniere when the moment comes."

"Then our help will be the more welcome," said Red. "Come back with us."

"Not I," said Pierre. "I have my own affairs to worry about. It makes no difference to me who rules; let them fight it out between them."

"You've changed," said Red sadly.

"You have to look after yourself in this world," snapped Pierre angrily. "No one else will do it for me, you know. You two can go and get yourself killed for Laudonniere's sweet sake if you like; I'm off back to Edelano."

He turned his back on us and starting fussing with the stuff he had been carrying down to the canoe when we arrived. Red hesitated a moment and I could see that the parting disturbed him. Pierre had been our friend; we had faced an unknown continent together; it would be sad for it all to end like this.

"Pierre," said Red gently, walking a few steps back towards the boats. "We have plenty of time, Pierre. Tell us about your success on your island." He tried to make his voice sound careless and easy but without quite succeeding.

Pierre did not show he had heard. He pushed his canoe down to the water, launched it and jumped aboard. He settled himself down, Indian fashion, on his knees, hesitated a moment as if about to change his mind, and then drove his paddle deep into the water and sent the canoe shooting out into the stream. He did not look back.

Red shrugged his shoulders and turned to me. "Poor Pierre," he said. "In a little while he will begin to feel very lonely."

"Perhaps being mayor of Le Havre will make up for that," I said, but I knew that it would not. Nothing is worse than being quite alone. I had known the feeling myself before I met Red and Pierre in Le Havre; to have no one in the whole world to think of you, pray for you, wish you well. It was almost like not existing.

We walked slowly and silently into the fort, and somehow the loss of Pierre Gambi seemed to draw us closer together. Red must have felt the same for, when we were standing in the square he suddenly put his arm round my shoulders and gave me a great hug.

"Let's go and see Arlac first," he said, "and cheer ourselves up."

2

Arlac made much of us and insisted on having a detailed account of all we had done at the farm. When, in our turn, we questioned him about the dissatisfaction in the fort he made light of it. "They are so many bags of wind," he said, "these Fourneaux. I have come across their sort before. If they make trouble—and I suppose they are going to if they can—we shall get over it easily enough. It is not a thing to be afraid of."

"Pierre Gambi was afraid of it," I said bitterly.

"No, not afraid," said Red gravely. "One must be fair. Selfish and misguided, perhaps, but not afraid."

"So you have seen our bright friend," laughed Arlac. "He came to see me, too. How he was full of himself! Such a story I could hardly believe."

"We didn't get as far as the story," said Red.

"Oh, but it was wonderful," said Arlac. "It seems he has got himself accepted by some native tribe living on an island. It is some way up the river, I gathered; in the middle of a sort of marsh and not much visited by other tribes, so that the chief is practically independent. Gambi had the luck—or the brilliance—to save the life of the chief's only daughter. Then he married her and was accepted by the tribe as the heir to the chief. This chief is an old man so Pierre, if he stays long enough, will be chief himself soon. What a strange boy that is!"

"But he spoke about wealth," I said. "Alligator skins particularly."

"Ah, yes, that is the thing," said Arlac. "This tribe is poor in everything except alligators. And the alligator is their god. They worship the creature and are forbidden to kill it so that the island is surrounded by hundreds and hundreds of the beasts. All except the chief and his family. The chief is also the priest, and he may kill the alligator as he wishes in order to use the skin for his house and clothing. And Pierre is one of the chief's family now, and is making a great slaughter."

"He says he will get a thousand skins and then return to France and be the mayor of Le Havre," I said.

"He also says," said Arlac, "that he will civilize the Indian tribe before he leaves. I wonder what he means by that?"

"He will only do good to himself," said Red morosely.

"Oh, come," laughed Arlac. "He is a comical fellow, your Pierre Gambi. You mustn't be so hard on him."

But Red was quite serious and refused to share Arlac's amusement. "No," he said firmly, "it is easy to laugh, but in fact Pierre is a robber and a brigand. He is plundering the Indians, upsetting their ways of living and giving them nothing in exchange. Most of us here are no better. This expedition was intended to build a colony; a sanctuary for those who were persecuted for their beliefs in France. We could have done that without hurting the native people here, but instead we have made enemies all round through a stupid and greedy search for gold. Pierre Gambi represents the worst features of the colony called Fort Caroline."

"And you, my friend," said Arlac warmly, "represent the best. You make me ashamed."

3

We reported to Laudonniere the following morning, having spent the rest of the previous afternoon and evening talking to Le Moyne, La Caille, Ottigny and others in an attempt to find out the seriousness of the conspiracy against Laudonniere. We discovered very little, however; whatever was brewing was being kept a close secret.

Laudonniere received us with rather wan pleasure. He asked a few questions about our success in our farming venture but seemed on the whole preoccupied with other thoughts. "I fear it is too late," he muttered, more to himself than to us.

"Too late, sir?" asked Red.

"The question of food for the fort will soon be critical,"

answered Laudonniere. "I greatly doubt if Saturiba can be persuaded to supply us for another year. I have been very foolish, I'm afraid. I should have had people like you out on the land as soon as we arrived, then we should be secure against this sort of trouble. Now I can only pray that Ribaut sends the relief boats very soon."

We talked on for a little while. Red made one of two oblique references to the trouble with Fourneaux and his followers. At first Laudonniere seemed not to understand, and then when he realized what Red was trying to say he quickly straightened his shoulders and his face took on an expression both haughty and insolent.

"Tell me, my boy," he drawled in that insolent tone that always showed him least sure of himself, "if it came to a fight, how many could I ... do you think ... how many would stand by me?"

"Scarcely half a dozen, sir," said Red, telling the brutal truth.

The bubble of Laudonniere's pose was pricked immediately. He hid his face in his hands and began to rock backwards and forwards on his chair, muttering words we could neither catch nor understand. When he looked up again his face had so changed that I pitied him deeply.

"Can you tell me why?" he asked, barely above a whisper.

Red and I exchanged glances. I said, "I can only repeat what we have heard men say. As you know we have been out of the fort ..."

"Well?" said Laudonniere sharply.

"They say you have only eyes for the past, and that you have proved from it, to your own satisfaction, that the expedition must fail, and that therefore you make no attempt to lead us to success. Le Moyne says that a leader should only look to the past to correct old errors..."

"Le Moyne?" cried Laudonniere, seizing on the name. "Is he one of my enemies now?"

"No," I said. "He is your friend. Else I should not have mentioned him."

"Friend or enemy," muttered Laudonniere, "he speaks with very pointed wisdom."

He sat, with his chin in his hands, for a long time after that, seeming not to notice us, and we were on the point of leaving quietly when there was a sudden, impatient thumping on the outer door, and before any answer could be made to it Sergeant La Caille came stamping in.

"What is this?" cried Laudonniere in a high-pitched and angry voice. "How dare you walk into my rooms without permission—"

"There is no time for courtesies," La Caille interrupted roughly. "You must come at once if any good is to be done. And even then I fear it may be too late."

"Come where? What are you talking about?"

"There is a meeting in the square and I have been sent to fetch you. They have elected me their spokesman—"

"So!" cried Laudonniere, "you are not only my enemy now, but the leader of my enemies?"

"Spokesman," corrected La Caille gravely. "I allowed myself to be chosen because I thought I might be able to moderate their demands. But as to being their leader... well, that hypocrite Fourneaux is their leader."

"Is this another mutiny?" demanded Laudonniere. "They say that history repeats itself..."

"History repeats itself when leaders go on making the same mistakes," said La Caille quietly. "However, it has not come to that yet, and your appearance in the square now may be sufficient."

They hurried out into the sun-baked square with Red and me close at their heels. Thirty or so of the settlers were standing or sitting in small groups waiting for something. Directly Laudonniere appeared they crowded round him with a loud angry hum; much the sound bees make when a hive is overturned. La Caille quickly called them to order.

"You have made me your spokesman," he shouted. "Then we will do the thing as it should be done; I will speak your demands."

I heard Laudonniere mutter the word, "demands" to himself with an indignant expression.

La Caille turned to Laudonniere. "You must understand, sir," he said earnestly, "that what I say now is said through me. I am not a party to this . . . this revolt."

"Very well," said Laudonniere wearily, and waved a tired hand as if he were brushing away a fly. "Say what has to be said, Sergeant, and let us get it over."

La Caille cleared his throat and launched himself into a long and involved speech, full of pompous words and complicated sentences that never seemed to reach a conclusion. "Sir," he said, "all of us here agree in recognizing you as the lieutenant of the King, our supreme lord in this province, where our present settlement has been founded in his name."

Laudonniere nodded absent-mindedly at this and glanced round as if seeking somewhere to rest.

"We will obey your orders on this honorable expedition," went on La Caille, "even if, for His Majesty's sake, we should have to sacrifice our lives. Yet..."

Here La Caille paused as if waiting for everyone's full attention. "Yet," he repeated emphatically, "we must respectfully remind you that before leaving France we were assured that provisions enough for a full year would be brought and that additional supplies would be at hand before these were exhausted. But far from this being the case, the provisions brought were scarcely enough for one month."

There was a murmur of agreement from the settlers at this and a great deal of head-wagging. Laudonniere was looking down at the ground scraping gently and persistently at the hard-baked earth with the toe of his boot.

La Caille went on to tell what all knew; how the Indians had at first supplied the lack of provisions but how, after a time, they had been antagonized by the behavior of the settlers and had withdrawn their help. The settlers, said La Caille, were now on the verge of starvation. There was an angry muttering from the crowd as he said this and the sergeant had to wait some moments for the noise to subside so that he could go on.

"In order to remedy this," he continued at last, "we all here most urgently beseech you to repair and refit one of the ships that brought us from France and is now lying in the river. We ask you to send her to nearby New Spain to obtain supplies by purchase... or otherwise."

La Caille had left a long pause after the word "purchase" and Laudonniere looked up with a frown and seemed on the point of speaking. La Caille hurried to a conclusion.

"We are sure that such a course would relieve us," he

said, "but if you have any better measures to suggest we are ready to agree to them."

There was a long silence. The crowd looked expectantly at Laudonniere who seemed to be staring over their heads at the distant palm trees on the bank of the river.

"Is that all?" he said ironically.

There was a brisk movement in the crowd and Fourneaux thrust himself to the front. "What about Gièvre?" he cried hoarsely. "You have said nothing about that!"

Laudonniere ignored him and turned to La Caille. "Purchase, or otherwise?" he said. "What is meant by this ... otherwise?"

La Caille looked embarrassed, and before he could answer Fourneaux shouted out, "Piracy! That's what! Take what we need from the Spaniards!"

"And you ask this seriously?" said Laudonniere. "Do you imagine I can give you permission to stir up trouble with Spain? What if it should lead to war? The idea is quite ridiculous. No ship under my charge will sail to New Spain, either on trade or ... the other thing."

There was an angry outburst from the men at this, all shouting at once and waving their arms, and it was some time before La Caille could command silence to speak again. "We have not finished!" he kept shouting. "There is more to come."

At last, when the noise had sunk to an undertone of muttered grumbles, Laudonniere spoke again.

"Hear me speak then," he cried. "You have put your case; here is my answer. In the first place, I am a soldier with orders to carry out and with responsibilities laid on me by His Majesty through the Constable of France. I will not be called to account for my actions by those in my charge. This meeting itself is a revolt against His Majesty's authority and you would all suffer were I to report it. However, if it goes no farther than this I shall take no action.... As for your ... requests ... I have two suggestions to make. First, I have a small reserve of trading stores which I will have shared among you if you wish. With these stores you may be able to regain the confidence of what Indians remain in the district. Second, the two shallops made by our carpenters, sailing ships large enough to carry half a dozen men each, will be available to you. With them you may run down the coast to the first Spanish settlement and either beg or buy supplies. You will be too few to embark on any violent means ... which is why I permit the use of the shallops but not of the ship.

"Well, that is all I have to say. Discuss the matter among yourselves if you wish. You will gain nothing by going on with this mutiny ... except your own punishment when the next ship arrives from France. When you have regained your senses you may send your spokesman to me again. That is my last word."

And with this, uttered in the haughtiest possible tone, Laudonniere turned his back on the angry settlers and stalked away. La Caille stood uncertainly for a few moments, first looking after Laudonniere and then glancing back at the group of men as if he were not at all sure what to do. Finally he too turned away from them and went to his quarters. Red and I hurried after Laudonniere, reaching his door only a few seconds after him.

4

Laudonniere took to his bed, as might have been expected, and stayed there for the rest of the day. There was nothing for me to do but stay somewhere near him in case I was needed. Once he asked for Ottigny and I went out into the fort to find him. But Ottigny and Arlac had both gone off with small parties of soldiers in an attempt to get food. When the sun went down they had still not returned.

With the darkness absolute silence fell over the fort. There were no lights to be seen anywhere, and no movement. Usually one could hear the tramp of sentries' feet and the occasional rattle of an arquebus, coughing, a little murmuring here and there where sentries met at the ends of their beats and laughter and sometimes songs from the soldiers' quarters. But tonight there was none of this. Only silence and stillness within the fort, and from outside in the forest the faint hum and whirr of insects and the occasional squawk of parrots disturbed on their branches. There was little else living in the nearby forest, for the game had all been killed for food or frightened away.

For some time I sat outside, crouched beside the open door, watching the faint flickering of lightning far away on the tops of the mountains. It was a warm, close night. My skin was sticky with undried sweat and my clothing felt uncomfortable. I was more bored with having nothing to do than anxious about the situation that had developed among the men.

All at once it occurred to me that it would be a good time to take a swim in the river. It was forbidden to leave the fort after dark, and it was never very safe to bathe in the river. But no sentries seemed to have been posted and I felt like taking advantage of the fact.

At least it would be something to do.

I crept back into Laudonniere's room to see if he was sleeping, but he was lying on his side with his eye watching the door.

"Well?" he said.

"I thought I would go and see if Lieutenant Ottigny was back yet," I said.

"Yes," he said. "Yes, go and see."

I went quickly, not down to Ottigny's quarters, but to Arlac's where I supposed Red would be. There was no sign of him, however, and I thought he had gone off with the others to get food. I felt rather lonely and deserted and wished we were back on the farm. The idea of a swim recurred to me and although I was less eager to go by myself, some stubborn streak pushed me on. I went down to that part of the fort wall overlooking the strand. There was a tunnel here constructed under the wall; a sort of sally port intended for use against Indians should they try to tamper with the boats; and I thought it would be easier and quieter to slip out this way than try to open one of the gates.

I went quietly, avoiding the open space in the center of the fort. The moon was still very low in the trees and there was little danger of my being seen unless I showed my outline against the sky, and this I was careful not to do. The tunnel was unguarded, and I crept through it and out on to the strand without any trouble. The two shallops were lying beached there, masts aslant against the sky, and by them some half a dozen Indian canoes that had been obtained at one time or another from the natives.

Standing close in to one of the shallops I stripped off my clothes, arranged them in a neat heap, and then, feeling a couple of rain spots on my bare back, pushed the heap close against the keel of the shallop where the bulging sides formed a sort of shelter.

The slow-moving water was tepid but refreshing, and I floated for some time just off the shore giving a few gentle kicks now and then when the current had drifted me too far past the boats. But the sound of a splash on the far bank suddenly reminded me of alligators and water snakes and I scrambled hastily ashore and went back to my clothes.

"Who's that?" cried a startled voice. I recognized it immediately as that of La Caille.

"It's all right," I said. "Only me—Pierre Debré."

"What the blazes are you doing here?" demanded La Caille sharply. I could see him now, bending over one of the canoes.

"I was only taking a little swim," I said. "I thought I needed to cool off after the fuss and bother of the afternoon."

"You know very well you are not allowed out of the fort after sunset," he said, and then laughed as he realized the absurdity of what he had said. "Fuss and bother, eh?" he went on. "It was a bit more than that, my lad, as you'll soon find out."

"How do you mean?" I said, struggling quickly into my clothes as I spoke.

"Throat-cutting sort of fuss and bother, that's what I mean," he said grimly.

"My throat?" I said.

"Maybe," he replied. "But mine for certain. That's why you find me in this undignified situation."

"You're running away!" I said, beginning to understand.

He grunted for an answer and began to haul the canoe down towards the water's edge. I went to help him.

"Yes," he said, when the prow of the canoe was afloat. "I got it from Le Moyne not more than a few minutes ago. They've been holding a meeting and it's all cut and dried now. Fourneaux is to take over leadership. They're off to be pirates, that's about the size of it. And anybody that tries to stop them will have his throat cut. Le Moyne says they were going to cut mine first as an example."

"But we must stop them," I exclaimed. "If they are disarmed—"

La Caille laughed abruptly, checking himself suddenly as he realized what a noise he had made. "Who's going to stop them," he said. "Tell me that, young fellow?"

"Well, you," I said. "And the soldiers."

"Sixty or more of the soldiers and all the officers have gone over to the rebels," said La Caille. "That leaves Ottigny, Arlac and myself, Le Moyne and perhaps a handful of men who are out of the fort . . ."

"And Laudonniere," I said.

"Who's lying in his bed sucking his thumb," said La Caille contemptuously. "Well, anyway, I'm not waiting here to be murdered. I'm going to try to get back to the ships and bring a dozen or so sailors back. I only hope I'll be in time, that's all."

"I'll come with you," I said quickly.

"That you won't," he replied fiercely. "You'll go

straight back to Laudonniere and tell him what I've just told you. Then you can try to intercept Ottigny and his hunting party before they return, and warn them. We've just a chance."

And before I could say anything La Caille pushed the canoe off into the stream and jumped in.

5

I am not, on the whole, a coward. It occurred to me that I could easily follow La Caille in one of the many canoes lying about on the strand. It occurred to me, too, that I could make my way through the forest to our cabin and be out of harm's way there, if I wished. Nevertheless I turned my back on the river and went back through the tunnel to warn Laudonniere.

I might have saved my courage for another occasion, for no sooner had I emerged into the fort than two soldiers jumped on me and carried me off to the barracks, which had become the headquarters of the rebels, and presented me to Fourneaux.

"We thought it was La Caille," they said. "He was coming up the sally port from the beach and we grabbed him."

"Good," said Fourneaux. "I'll deal with him. You can get back to your posts."

The two soldiers marched off leaving me standing before what I took to be the committee of the rebellion. The barrack room had been rearranged to suit its new purpose. All the bunks had been cleared back to the walls and the center of the floor was empty except for a small table at which sat three men. In the center, facing me, was Fourneaux; on his right an Italian from Genoa called Stephen; on his left a bumptious little Gascon called Seignore, an officer who had been promoted from the ranks. This last man had a sort of greenish complexion, the result I believe of some internal disorder, and when he swelled himself up, puffing out his cheeks and his fleshy neck, he looked exactly like one of those silly green marsh frogs.

"Well?" said Seignore, banging his fist on the table, "what have you got to say for yourself? What were you doing down on the beach?"

"Swimming," I said.

The little man jumped to his feet and running round the table stood close up to me quivering with rage. "Have a care!" he screamed.

"But I *was* swimming," I said.

Seignore raised himself on his toes until he was about the same height as myself. I thought for a moment that he was going to strike me, but instead he spat in a spluttering sort of way in my face and then, apparently satisfied, went back to the table and sat down again.

Fourneaux tapped gently on the table waiting. Then he leaned forward and said in that gentle, oily voice, "And was La Caille also on the beach?"

"If he was I didn't see him," I lied.

Fourneaux seemed satisfied with this for he went straight on, "And who is with Laudonniere?"

"No one," I said.

"Where is Ottigny, then?"

"I don't know."

"Arlac?"

"I don't know."

The three men looked at me for a few seconds and then turned to each other. "What shall we do with him?" said Fourneax. Stephen shrugged his shoulders. Seignore seemed on the point of saying something when Fourneaux added quietly, "Of course, we don't want to use any *unnecessary* violence. And after all, the boy is quite harmless...."

Stephen of Genoa shrugged again, fiddling all the time with a small poignard, splintering the table-top. "Let him go, then," he said carelessly. "After midnight, of course."

They all seemed agreed on this and I was sent to the very end of the barrack room farthest from the door and permitted to lie on one of the bunks. I chose one with a splendid robe of matched deerskin thrown across it and lay there for some time, dozing and waking again. Whenever I opened my eyes the three men were still leaning over their table with their heads close together murmuring, planning I knew not what.

At some time during the night the rain that had been threatening all the evening suddenly broke on us. I awoke with a start to hear the water hammering on the roof. Within a few minutes all the men had come in, wet through even in that short time.

For half an hour or more the rain kept up a steady roar on the wooden roof. The men were shouting at each other to make themselves heard, and even then their voices hardly carried across the barrack room. Now and again they would fall silent and listen with awed looks on their faces to the sounds outside and then quickly fall to talking again as if the clatter of their tongues were a protection against the storm and the rising river.

I dozed off, lulled by the sounds of wind and water,

woke and dozed again and then came wide awake and refreshed. The rain had ceased outside. Most of the men in the barrack room were nodding off in the close atmosphere; even Fourneaux slept slumped on the table with his head on his arms. The objectionable Gascon was nowhere to be seen. Stephen of Genoa leaned back in his chair with folded arms, watching the room through half-closed eyelids.

I got quietly up off the bed and walked down the length of the barrack room towards the door. It seemed at least a mile away. I tried to walk casually but I was so keyed up with fear that I felt blown up with the blood my heart was pumping. My head ached with the pressure and there was a noise like frying fat in my ears. No matter how I tried I could not walk in a straight line down the side of the room. The room itself seemed to be prancing about around me.

One man, half-asleep by the side of the door, sprawled across the way, saw me coming and drew his feet in. I wanted to burst out laughing at the absurdity of it. Then Stephen's voice came drowsily from the other end of the room: "Where's the boy off to?"

I turned without a thought in my head as to what I should say, but some words formed by themselves. Quite pointless words. I said, "I must go outside for a moment ... the fresh air."

"Feel sick, lad?" asked another voice.

I nodded and then hurried the last few steps to the door, almost running. Stephen's voice came again, more awake this time, as if he had half guessed at my intention.

"Jacques!" he said sharply. "Go with the boy. Keep an eye on him."

I went on out, almost falling down the steps. A voice from inside told me to wait and hurried footsteps made for the door. I had no time at all in which to disappear, and the moon was just coming out of the edge of a ragged cloud. Then, just as the door began to open again, I turned, saw the dark hole under the steps, and dived in.

I landed on my face in mud and water and lay there, half-choked and trembling, as the feet went over me like thunder.

"He's gone!" cried a voice.

The barrack room came to life immediately. Men shouted at one another, ran here and there, gave orders, cursed and swore as they ran into one another in the dark.

"Get a torch!" shouted someone.

I knew that sooner or later it would occur to one of them that I couldn't have gone far, and then they would search closer and find me. I slid backwards, away from the steps and right under the barrack room itself. It was raised off the ground by something less than two feet, and by wriggling forward on my chest and pushing hard with my toes I managed to keep moving. The mud collected against my shoulders gradually mounting up to form a barrier, and I had to stop every few yards to clear a way for myself.

I pushed on for what seemed a long while in the pitch dark, not knowing where I was going. But eventually a thin line of moonlight reflected on the liquid mud showed me the end of the barracks, and a few moments later I emerged at the far end not more than twenty yards from the inner wall of the fort. I lay still in the shadow wondering what action I ought to take. There seemed a good chance of getting right round the outside of the fort in time to catch Ottigny and his soldiers before they returned to the fort. Whether that would make a large enough party to overthrow the mutineers I could not say, but it was worth a try.

And then, at the very point of deciding on this action, I heard the sound of the main gate opening, of Ottigny's voice giving orders. There was no time left for subtleties. I got to my feet and raced across the open barrack square as hard as I could go, slipping and floundering in the mud, expecting at any moment to get an arquebus ball in the back. In the moonlight I could clearly make out the figures of Ottigny, Arlac and Red standing by the gate which the soldiers were closing. They were in the act of dropping the bar across when I reached them.

"Open the gate again," I panted. "Quick. The mutiny!" I had no breath left for more but stood panting in front of them with my lips moving but no words coming from my mouth. They did not recognize me, of course, as I was covered from head to foot with mud.

"Open it!" I shrieked, suddening getting my voice back. "Fourneaux is leading a mutiny—"

"It sounds like Pierre," exclaimed Red taking a step towards me.

I waved my arms wildly at him so that the eagle sitting on his shoulder mantled suddenly, and then I saw that it was no use and dropped my arms to my sides again. All that for nothing. Coming out from either side of the gateway were a dozen or more men, walking cautiously, their leveled crossbows aimed at the two officers. Of course that was why the men were waiting in the barrack room; that was why the beginning of the mutiny had been so strangely delayed. They had set a trap at the gate and were waiting for the victims to walk into it.

Ottigny heard something and spun round, his sword already half out of its scabbard, but Red reached out and held his arm. It was pointless to resist.

Directed by one of the soldiers, we turned and went across the square to the barrack room where the committee of three, now fully awake, were waiting for us. Stephen of Genoa grinned when he saw me but said nothing.

Ottigny looked at the three leaders contemptuously. "What is this foolishness?" he demanded angrily.

"No foolishness at all," said Fourneaux calmly. "You know that Laudonniere refused us the use of a ship. Despite his refusal we are taking one, and to make sure that no one tries to stop us we are taking the precaution of locking all the officers in their quarters for the rest of the night."

"We do not wish to harm anyone," added Stephen of Genoa. "If you would be good enough to surrender your arms and go quietly to your cabin you will not be touched."

Ottigny and Arlac stood defiantly in the center of the room glaring round at the circle of faces. There was a tense moment when we were all, I think, very near to death, and during which, I am not too proud to admit, I was profoundly afraid. Then Ottigny unbuckled his belt and let the sword and scabbard clatter to the ground, and the other imitated his example. There was an audible sigh of relief, and then Stephen said gently, "Thank you. And now, gentlemen...."

We turned as if in a dream towards the door. Ottigny went out with two soldiers, and Arlac followed.

"Now you," said a soldier to Red and put a hand on his arm. What followed was almost too quick to be seen. The eagle on Red's shoulder struck at the man, ripping his sleeve from elbow to wrist and gouging at the flesh beneath. The man sprang back with a yell.

"I am very sorry," said Red gently, "but there was no need to touch me." And he turned and walked out.

"Not you!" said Stephen, pointing at me. "You are to go with us."

"Where to?" I asked, fearing that perhaps my earlier attempt to escape was now going to be punished.

"To depose King Laudonniere," said Fourneaux with a laugh.

"But why take me?"

"We need a witness to a document he is going to sign," said Fourneaux. "And besides, he'll need a shoulder to cry on afterwards. Come along!"

6

Fourneaux did not mean to take any chances. He took a party of twenty arquebusiers with him to Laudonniere's cabin. Ten of them stood about outside the doors and windows to prevent any escape, the rest followed Fourneaux in.

Laudonniere was lying on his bed as we entered, awake and staring at the door. He sat up quickly when the soldiers tramped into the room, but before he had time to speak or reach for a weapon Fourneaux was upon him and was holding the naked edge of a sword against his throat.

Laudonniere showed no fear; only a sort of cold curiosity. "Well," he said, "there was a fine dramatic touch to your entrance. How does the play proceed? Is it to be a comedy, or a tragedy, I wonder?"

"That depends on you," said Fourneaux grimly and motioned to one of the men who had come prepared with a heavy set of leg irons. Laudonniere allowed these to be fixed to his ankles without protest, only glancing down at them when the work was finished and giving a slight shrug of the shoulders.

"Well," he said, "now the wolf is penned, the sheep may eat the grass, eh? I suppose you will all run off now and try your luck against the Spaniards. What fools you are!"

"That's enough of that," said Fourneaux roughly, afraid perhaps that Laudonniere's tongue would influence the soldiers. "We've come for two things, and then our business is over as far as you're concerned. First, the keys of the armory and the stores!"

Laudonniere took the keys from his belt and handed them over as calmly as if he were passing the salt. "And the other thing?" he said.

Fourneaux took from his pouch a small roll of parchment and passed it to Laudonniere. "Read that," he commanded. "Read it, and sign it!"

Laudonniere quickly looked through the document with an amused smile. "Very childish," he commented when he had read it.

"Sign it!" said Fourneaux angrily.

"Do you imagine for one instant that this will protect you from just punishment?" asked Laudonniere.

"Sign it!" shouted Fourneaux.

Laudonniere held the document up and read aloud from it: "I hereby appoint the following officers, namely Fourneaux, Stephen of Genoa, Seignore and La Croix, to proceed with an adequate party to New Spain, and there to demand, or enforce, as they see fit, assistance from the inhabitants."

Fourneaux seized a pen from the writing table, dipped it deep in the inkwell and held it out. Laudonniere took it with a polite nod and signed his name at the foot of the document. I signed beneath as witness. As he returned the paper he remarked, "I think that is one of the best jokes I have ever taken part in. However, if you can get any comfort from it . . ."

Fourneaux ignored him and began to order the soldiers outside. At the door he turned. "There will be a guard set outside," he said, "with instructions to shoot anyone leaving this cabin. Some time tomorrow you will be set free . . . I don't think we shall meet again."

"The thought fills me with sorrow," said Laudonniere gravely.

Fourneaux was wrong, as it turned out, but the circumstances of their next meeting must keep for another chapter.

7

After leaving Laudonniere the mutineers opened up the armory and the store, took all the weapons in the fort and most of the remaining food and went off down river in the two shallops. They did not, in the end, attempt to seize one of the ships. No armed men were left, but this was not discovered until the following morning when Ottigny ventured out of his cabin and found the fort deserted. The colonists, who on the whole had remained passive, had been disarmed and locked up in their several quarters. Those who lived outside the fort knew nothing of the business from start to finish.

La Caille returned soon after daybreak with twenty sailors from the ships. He had come by land and missed the mutineers. By that time Ottigny had released Laudonniere and the fort had resumed its normal day-to-day activity. Laudonniere must have decided not to inquire too closely into the activities of the various people who still remained. A roll was called and the absent men, sixty-eight of them altogether, were stigmatized as rebels and outlaws.

The rebellion had one good result; it seemed to cure Laudonniere completely of his ill-health. From that point onward he was active in running the life of the fort in an orderly and conscientious way.

During the months that followed we learned, bit by bit, what had happened to the rebels in their two shallops. We got most of the story from deserters who began to return to the fort in ones and twos. Altogether eight men came back, threw themselves on Laudonniere's mercy and were generously forgiven. From them we were able to gather what had happened.

It seemed that the shallops under Fourneaux's command had at first excellent luck. They sailed south until they were off the island of Cuba, and there they met with a small trading ship, a brigantine, carrying wine to the Spanish colonies. They captured the ship without much difficulty and almost immediately afterwards fell in with a larger and better provisioned Portuguese caravel. This they captured also.

They were now, as one of the deserters put it, well set up in business. They had two ships and two shallops with a plentiful supply of food and drink. Indeed they had rather more wine than was good for them, and this seems to have been their undoing. Made bold by their remarkable success, they then landed on the island of Jamaica where they captured a village and lived like lords for a week or more. When word came to them that the governor of the island was cruising off the coast, instead of slipping quietly away they embarked in their little fleet and sailed out to attack the lonely vessel.

A fight followed. Eventually the pirates captured the governor and his ship, and nothing would satisfy them until they had ransomed the poor man for a fortune.

The governor, however, was not so stupid as they thought. He sent his son ashore with a letter to his wife asking for the ransom—the pirates read the letter first and suspected no trickery—and also with private instructions to his secretary.

At daybreak the next day the simple, unsuspecting pirates were amazed to see three heavily armed warships sailing out from the island. They tried to run but the enemy was faster. They were overtaken and in the fight that followed all the pirates were either killed or captured.

This was as far as our knowledge of the story went until some weeks later, towards the end of March in the third year of the life of the colony.

Word reached the fort, from some passing Indians who

had been trading down the river, that a large vessel had been sailing up and down outside the mouth of the river for two or three days. Everyone was greatly excited at the news. At first we thought it must be the relief ship from France, now long overdue. Then our excitement turned to fear when someone suggested it might be a Spanish man-of-war seeking revenge for the piratical raids of Fourneaux and his men.

In the end Laudonniere sent a small party down the river to reconnoiter and it was discovered that the ship was the same brigantine captured by the pirates, and now manned by twenty or more of them. They had somehow or other contrived to escape from Jamaica, and after cruising up and down the coast for some days without success were now on the point of starvation. It seemed they were ready to make terms with Laudonniere and return to the fort.

Laudonniere was suspicious. The business of the colony had gone on so much better without the malcontents that he was not overanxious to have any of them back. On the other hand the colony was sorely in need of a ship. In the end he sent La Caille down the river in a new shallop the carpenter had lately completed; La Caille and a crew of two, but with thirty armed men concealed in the bottom of the boat under an old sailcloth.

The pirates were starving but drunk—there were still casks of wine unopened in the hold, but not a scrap of food—and they were easily captured and brought up to the fort. Fourneaux was among them, and the Genoese, Stephen. La Croix and Seignore had been killed in the battle with the Spaniards.

Laudonniere acted quickly. A court-martial was held

within an hour of the arrival of the prisoners. All twenty-six men were found guilty. Fourneaux and Stephen were condemned to death, the remainder were released on an oath of loyalty and good behavior. The execution of the two leaders took place at sunset that same day.

So ended the mutiny.

Chapter Six

STARVATION

As I have already said, Laudonniere was a changed man after the affair of the mutiny. He seemed suddenly to become a true leader. A little late in the day, some of the more cynical said, but nevertheless even they had to admit that the small amounts of food that trickled into the fort from that time onwards would have stopped altogether but for Laudonniere's efforts.

Red and I had returned to our farm almost immediately after the mutiny. We were not there when the mutineers returned, were tried and dealt with, because we were busy with our first harvest. The maize we had planted had done very well indeed; the seed corn brought from France gave a fair yield, but with the difference in soil and climate having a different effect on the plant, it did not grind down into a good flour. It was too pulpy and soft and made a heavy, tasteless bread. It was clear that this Indian corn, the maize, was the best crop to grow for the present. The other farmers who had left the fort at the same time as Red and I had been less experimental. One of them had tried a sort of native pumpkin which had done well. This was delightful to eat, having a sweet flavor and juicy flesh, but it was not much use to a hungry man.

About this time Laudonniere sent out word that he wanted all the settlers in outlying farms to go in to the fort to see him when their harvests were carried. By this time there were fourteen men farming outside the fort. They were all there when we arrived; having smaller harvests to carry they had finished sooner.

Laudonniere called a meeting in his quarters and put the situation honestly to us. He said that the fort was on the very edge of starvation now. Saturiba had refused further supplies of food ten days before; the last barrel of flour in the store brought from France had been opened that morning.

"The colony," he said, "is now entirely dependent on its own resources, and those resources are the hunting ability of our soldiers and the food produced on our farms."

He then asked us in turn for a true figure regarding the harvest brought in. We gave him our answers and he noted them down. After a few minutes, during which the only sound in the room was the scratching of his pen and the creaking of the chairs we sat fidgeting in, he arrived at a total. It was ridiculously inadequate. Between us we had grown enough food to last the colony forty-three days.

"Perhaps the relief ship will arrive before that," he said, but his voice did not sound as if he believed this.

"You wish to take all our crops?" said one of the farmers.

"I must," said Laudonniere. "After you have taken your seed for next year, and the bare minimum to last you round . . . I must have it. We are in a desperate situation."

No one mentioned that the original agreement had been to supply the fort with a fixed fraction of the harvest; no one asked why fourteen farmers had to feed more than a hundred idle noblemen. When the meeting finished we were glad to get out of the mean atmosphere of the fort as quickly as possible.

2

During the next month or so Red and I were in and out of Fort Caroline every third or fourth day. There was little to do on the farm at this end of the year and Red insisted that we both spent every spare moment out hunting. We developed a system of trapping and snaring; we used both eagles to hunt birds; and we spent much time building a sturdy stockade to hold wild cattle. This last was Red's idea and so far nothing had come of it. The Indians had no domestic animals except a sort of half-wild dog, but they told many tales of herds of large cattle that came once a year through that territory, and which we thought might be captured and domesticated. "At the worst," said Red, "we could keep a few dozen of these creatures captive until we needed to kill them for food." The Indians had shown us rough drawings of these creatures and they seemed somewhat like our own cattle, but heavier in the shoulder and with a sort of thick mane.

Whenever we had a successful kill we carried it in to the fort. At first I protested against using the whole of our time in this way. There were dozens of idle soldiers well able to do the hunting, and meanwhile we were neglecting our farm. Red, however, would not listen to me.

"Don't you see," he said, "that if the fort goes, we go too. We are not strong enough to keep our farms without them. We have made friends with a few of the Indians near us, but we are still at the mercy of any wandering band. We must feed the fort. It is not only Christian charity; it is also good common sense."

All this time the man Gièvre lived with us at the farm. He was of very little use to us, having no desire to work and no love of farming. He seldom entered into our conversations but sat most of the time, glum and silent, as close to the fire as he could get. We ignored him in the end and went our own way as if he did not exist.

By now most of the Indians had moved out of the area. Apart from the small farming communities on the north of the river there remained now only one small tribe of river-dwelling Indians within reach of the fort. Laudonniere visited their chief personally and after presenting him with a number of gifts arranged that members of the tribe should recommence trading with the fort. These Indians were fisheaters and had nothing else to offer but the surplus of the daily catch. This fish was welcome enough but it was never in large enough quantities to solve the problem.

Finally, when even the newly harvested grain had almost disappeared, Laudonniere decided to send to Outina. As he said, the French had fought a battle for him; the least Outina could do was reward them with a gift of corn.

The party, six men under Arlac, sailed off and the fort waited with high hopes during the week that followed. When the returning boat was sighted far up the river the whole population turned out on the strand to greet it.

A groan of disappointment and rage went up as the men stepped ashore. The six soldiers were empty handed; Arlac carried a small wicker basket with merely a few pounds of maize in it, not enough for a handful for each man in the fort.

"What did he say?" demanded Laudonniere angrily, when he saw the corn.

"Outina says that he owes us nothing," said Arlac bitterly, "but he offers us another war."

"Another war?"

Arlac gave a faint smile. "It appears," he said, "that one of the petty chiefs under him has refused to pay the yearly tribute. Outina says that if we will march against the man and collect the tribute we may keep half of it for our pains."

Laudonniere spread his hands and appealed silently to the crowd.

"We are in no condition to fight," remarked La Caille looking along the ragged scarecrows of men that lined the wall of the fort.

Nevertheless the thought of food had excited the men. They shouted indignantly at La Caille, insisting that the offer be accepted.

STARVATION

Laudonniere shrugged his shoulders. "On your own heads be it," he muttered. And then aloud, "We will hold an inspection tomorrow morning. Only fit men will be chosen."

3

On the following morning the whole population of the fort turned out in the square. Laudonniere was soon there and close behind him came Ottigny carrying a large cooking cauldron and four soldiers each with a lead pig in his arms. Ottigny set the cauldron down in the center of the square and the soldiers dropped the lead pigs into it.

"Right," said Laudonniere. "Will those who wish to go on this expedition please step forward!"

About sixty men stepped forward immediately.

"Come forward in turn and lift this cauldron, holding it a hand's width clear of the ground for a slow count of ten," he ordered.

The men came forward self-consciously and took their turn at the handle of the cauldron. Some of them lifted it clear of the ground and held it without strain until Laudonniere had counted ten. Some of them barely managed to raise it and then let it go again with a gasp. And some failed to move it at all, so weak had they become after weeks of semistarvation.

Ottigny selected the men who had lifted the cauldron and made them stand apart from the others, and when the trial was over he had altogether twenty-four men, the strongest in the fort.

"This is the party then," announced Laudonniere. "Lieutenant Ottigny, you will lead them. Get arms from the armory and leave as soon as you are ready. And God be with you."

The lure of food was so great and the men themselves so eager to be gone that the party marched out of the fort within an hour.

For the next few days I cannot clearly tell how we continued to exist. I remember that one day the whole fort fed on a sort of bread made from dried fishbones—it seems to me comic now, but it was far from comic at the time. It began by one of the men talking in the evening of the comforts of his home back in France; this was a favorite topic of conversation in the evenings when we all sat round in one or other of the half-empty barrack rooms, too hungry to try to sleep.

This man began to talk of the huge quantities of food his uncle used to eat. His uncle was a farmer, apparently, and the speaker, as a boy, used to spend some part of the summer on the farm. He talked longingly of the ham, eggs, meat, fruit to be had in plenty.

"And yet," he said musingly, "my uncle was in many ways a careful man. Even mean. He could not abide anything to be wasted. Why, even the fishbones from Friday's dinner were dried in the sun and broken up for the fowls. 'It all comes back in eggs,' he used to say."

We were not really listening to the man and the conversation passed on to other topics and the gluttonous uncle was soon forgotten. But I suppose it must have started an idea in the man's head. Next morning he was out on the river bank with a basket collecting bits of sun-bleached fishbones. He put the whole lot through the small hand corn grinder and produced a pound or so of grayish-green flour and with this he made up three large, flat loaves. The smell when they were baking was horrible, but he kept them cooking until they were hard right through like a ship's biscuit.

By the time he took the loaves from under the fire he had a large, interested audience. We stood and watched as he broke one of the loaves in half and started to eat. At first he chewed doubtfully as if he found it unpleasant. Then he began to eat more and more quickly, stuffing the fragments into his mouth, dropping pieces on the ground in his haste, and all the time glancing round suspiciously as if he expected someone to rob him. That was enough: there was a mad rush for the river bank to collect fishbones.

4

While they were cooking their doubtful meal of fishbone bread, Red and I slipped out and returned to the farm. We felt guilty in the knowledge that there was still half a haunch of smoked venison hanging in the chimney and that we at least did not need to go hungry to bed. And yet, I reasoned, we had no cause for guilty feelings. We had done more than anyone else to relieve the situation at the fort. Nevertheless, we didn't talk much as we paddled down the river.

"I wonder how Gièvre is?" said Red as we made our way through the strip of forest between the farm and the river.

"Gièvre? I'd forgotten him," I said.

"We ought not to have protected him," said Red, speaking more to himself than to me. "The man is a troublemaker and an enemy of the colony. We ought to have sent him on his way."

"The laws of hospitality," I said. "I hope he has looked after the eagles."

The thought of Gièvre being in the cabin spoiled the rest of the journey for me. I had imagined lighting a fine log fire and stretching out before it as the evening came down, free from the worries of the fort. Before the mutiny I had been experimenting with weaving baskets, using a sort of osier that grew in the marshy land near the river. I had planned to try my hand at a sort of couch when I had the time.

"Perhaps he has gone," I said. "He will have been lonely by himself."

Red merely grunted.

As we neared the edge of the forest Red stood suddenly still in the middle of the track and sniffed. Immediately I realized that I had been smelling smoke for some time but had been too thoughtful to pay much attention to it. We both broke into a run without wasting breath to speak.

At the edge of the plain we stopped. "There was no need to hurry," said Red bitterly. "An hour ago would have been too late."

Before us the plain was a rolling mass of smoke. The wind was in our backs and was blowing both smoke and fire to the north so that we could see quite clearly something that we had both hoped not to see; the burned ruins of the cabin and the black stubble of the fields. High in the air were two wheeling specks that might have been our eagles.

The fire had caught the dried autumn grass of the

prairie and was already more than a mile away. It might burn for a hundred miles now before the wind dropped or a river crossed its line of advance. There was nothing we could do. We walked out to the blackened ruin that had been our home and as we drew near a man got up out of the grass and came to meet us. It was Gièvre. His eyes were wide with a sort of terror and his face was even whiter than usual. He babbled at us incoherently, waving his hands about but not saying anything that seemed to make sense.

Red pushed past him without a word and walked over the ashes of the cabin, kicking pieces of still-glowing wood aside and staring morosely at the ground. There was absolutely nothing left of any value; our stores, our seed corn, our clothing and cured animal skins, even the farm implements, all destroyed. I pushed at something among the ashes that showed gray among the black; it was the shoe of the plough—all that remained of it.

"We could make another plough," I said stupidly.

"Yes," said Red.

There didn't seem to be anything else to say.

Red stared around at the line of unburned ground to the south of the cabin. The cabin had only been a few yards inside the burned area.

"Look at that," he said. "It only just touched the cabin. We deserved better luck than that."

I saw the truth of it first. "The fire started *at* the cabin," I said. "The wind is from the south; it couldn't have reached the farm otherwise."

We both turned and stared at Gièvre who began to babble again, twisting his hands. He was trying to say something about the powder barrel. He said he thought it was empty. He threw it on the fire to save himself the trouble of collecting more firewood from the forest. He didn't know there was still some powder in the bottom.

It didn't seem to matter. We turned our backs on the man and walked away, back towards the river and our canoe and the starving fort. Far overhead the two specks circled once more and then swung off and were lost to sight. I thought I heard a thin faint scream like the scream of an eagle.

5

Red and I were now irrevocably back in the fort. There was no question of our trying to start again at the farm yet; the fort was starving, the whole colony was in danger of extinction, and there was nothing we could do now except share their fate one way or another.

And I had not realized how far the strength of the fort had been brought down. Red and I had gone hungry now and then but on the whole we had been feeding well during the previous six months and had built up strong healthy bodies. We were like giants compared with the people who had remained in the fort. Men we had known as powerfully built soldiers were now no more than tired, walking skeletons. On all sides we saw gray faces, yellow bloodshot eyes, weakness, weariness and a pervading apathy. No one any longer seemed to care what happened; no one made any effort to avert what was now felt to be certain tragedy.

For a couple of days Red and I walked about the fort appalled by what we saw. Then I decided to go to Laudonniere and resume serving him, while Red persuaded

STARVATION

half a dozen of the less weakened soldiers to go off with him on a hunting expedition. The only game now left in the forest consisted of small birds, reptiles and rodents, all too small to be worth arquebus fire. But Red made new snares and nets and instructed the soldiers in their use.

Some time after Red and his hunters had gone off the war party under Ottigny returned. They had been away ten days, and now they filed back into the fort with such an air of defeat that no one dared to question them. Ottigny stamped into Laudonniere's quarters and stood glaring at his superior. He was obviously in a furious temper, weary, spattered with blood and grime and with his clothing torn in many places. He had lost one boot and he limped as he walked, and he wore one shirt sleeve bound roughly round his knee as if he were wounded there.

"Ah," said Laudonniere, taking no apparent notice of his lieutenant's condition, "you are back then. What have you to report?"

Ottigny seemed to choke back something before he was able to speak, then he said in a hoarse, unnatural voice, "The village Outina wanted subdued was one in the middle of a marsh. He gave us no assistance whatever; not even a guide."

Laudonniere frowned in quick anger.

"It turned out to be a tiny, insignificant place of not more than twelve or fifteen huts," went on Ottigny. "The resistance was feeble and soon overcome."

"Good," said Laudonniere. "And the tribute?"

"Paid on the spot," said Ottigny. "Here is our share!" He opened a leather sack he had been carrying and turned it out on the floor. Out slithered half a dozen bright green snakes.

"The people of the village were snake eaters," he added.

Laudonniere sighed and turned his back on the creatures. "You have been put to great pain and trouble for nothing," he said.

Ottigny looked angrily at his chief's back. "At first they feared us, thinking us akin to gods," he muttered. "Then they got to know our weaknesses and hated us, but still with fear because of the power of our arquebuses."

"Well?" said Laudonniere, without turning round. "That is a natural order, I suppose."

"But now," went on Ottigny fiercely, "they despise us so much that they think they can mock at us. Outina must be taught a lesson. He must be shown that civilized Christian people, however few and however hungry, are still to be respected."

Laudonniere turned and looked at his officer curiously. "Should be taught, I agree," he said quietly. "But by whom? We are not strong enough to march out and take our revenge...."

"We may not be strong enough," cried Ottigny, "but by God we are angry enough!"

The upshot of the matter was that Laudonniere went across to the barrack rooms there and then to find out the temper of the settlement. Already the story of the expedition and of Outina's mockery had been told there and discussed and it was immediately obvious that the settlers were in a very ugly mood. Laudonniere had been unpopular for too long to wish to seek more unpopularity. He did not attempt to calm down the anger against

Outina, but instead listened to all that was said and kept his opinions to himself. At the end of it all he held up his hand for silence.

"It seems to me," he said calmly, "that this Indian barbarian must be taught a lesson."

During the wild cheers that greeted this I looked quickly at Ottigny to see how he was taking this change of face on Laudonniere's part. Even the phrase was Ottigny's own. But the lieutenant merely glanced at me out of the corner of his eye and gave the slightest quiver of an eyelid, and then turned and cheered with the rest. Laudonniere, I thought, was blessed with better officers than he deserved.

Laudonniere held up his hand again. "I shall lead the expedition myself," he declared. "We will capture Outina or members of his family, whichever is the more convenient, and ransom them for sacks of corn and shoulders of venison. What do you think of that?"

The storm of shouts and cheers that greeted this left no doubt as to the opinions of the settlers. And indeed it was a brilliant idea, for by connecting our hunger with our anger, Laudonniere had made sure of getting himself a large and willing army.

"Tomorrow at daybreak," he cried. "All men capable of bearing arms! Assemble in the square under your officers!"

6

Next day Laudonniere chose about a hundred men to go on the kidnaping raid. Of these he made a main party of sixty, a raiding party of twenty-five, and a reconnaissance party of fifteen. The main party was under the command of Sergeant La Caille, the raiding party under Laudonniere himself, and the reconnaissance party under Ottigny and Arlac. The reconnaissance party consisted of the fittest men and both Red and I were members of it. I must admit that this arrangement gave me secret amusement—and satisfaction. Six months before I had been looked on in the fort as something of a milksop. One grew up quickly in Florida, however; I was now a man, and thanks to Red and his farming, one of the fifteen strongest men in the fort. So much for the poor white creature that crawled out from under his printing press for a breath of fresh air not so very long ago.

The raid was planned to the last detail. Ottigny and Arlac knew Outina's village well, even down to the layout of the huts. Every man in the raiding and reconnaissance parties was given his particular place in the plan, his particular task. The main party had no part in the actual kidnaping. They were our defence line, and their task was to hold themselves in readiness to guard against Indian reprisals once the raid had been successfully accomplished.

7

Some time just before midnight our two shallops crept slowly up the river and came to anchorage in midstream about a quarter of a mile below the primitive jetty used by the Indians of Outina's village. Immediately, and in absolute silence, three canoes of the reconnaissance party threw off the tow lines that had been drawing them behind the leading ship and made for the bank. Our canoe contained Arlac, Red, a soldier named Bidon, a settler named La Pouce, and myself.

The other two canoes put straight into the bank and the ten men in them landed and disappeared silently into the shadow of the trees. We held on our course, going slowly against the current, and keeping about twenty feet out from the river bank. We made no effort to conceal ourselves.

This, for me, was the worst part of the whole raid. We were acting as decoys, and it gave one a very nasty feeling in the pit of the stomach to be wondering whether an arrow would come whistling out of the forest at any moment. We reached the jetty without incident and stood off from it, waiting for the signal from the land party. Their task was to approach the jetty from the land side and so block the escape of any sentries that might be guarding the jetty. There was no sound whatever except the natural small sounds of the night: the movement of water, the hum of insects and occasionally the discontented squawk of a bird moving its perch in the trees.

Then the signal came; a stone thrown from somewhere on the bank dropped into the water. It might have been a large fish rising to feed, but we knew that it wasn't. We lifted our paddles and glided in towards the end of the jetty. Almost at once there came the sound of a heron croaking. The sound seemed to come from under the jetty itself. It was answered by another heron a few yards up the river. Red stopped paddling and put his hand on Arlac's arm. Arlac turned and nodded. There was no need for words. Herons do not croak at one another in the middle of the night; the Indians had their signaling system too, it seemed.

The question now was whether there were enough Indians concealed around the jetty to try to repel us, or whether they would merely attempt to run off to the Indian camp with the warning that we were approaching. We were prepared for either action, but I felt horribly exposed in the canoe waiting to see what would happen next.

Then it happened quickly. The canoe touched the end of the jetty, Arlac swung himself up and then, like a cat, leaped to one side. There was a shrill whistle as an arrow went through the middle of the place where Arlac had been, and then a dark figure broke from the shadow of one of the timbers of the jetty, leaped ashore and ran, zigzagging across the open towards the dark of the wood.

Arlac did not move. It was all planned. The Indian ran straight at the darkness and disappeared, and almost immediately after there was the sound of a thud and a sort of choked gasp. Then silence again. Arlac nodded and we climbed out of the canoe and went down the jetty to the land. As we did so, the land party emerged from concealment in the edge of the forest carrying two Indians. They grinned but said nothing. One of the Indians, the one who had been hiding on the jetty itself, was unconscious; the other was conscious and very frightened. Both were bound and gagged. We left them, tied back to back on either side of a tree, and moved off towards the Indian camp.

The way, we knew, was an avenue that ran almost parallel to the river itself. Probably it had been at one time the original bed of the river, which would account for the way the trees grew on either side in lines, almost as if they had been planted. It was slightly sunken, too, below the level of the forest around. We went up this avenue with all possible caution, taking our time and keeping well in to the side in the dark shadow of the trees. We went, like the Indians themselves, soft-footed, slinking from tree to tree, and taking every advantage of cover that offered. Something at least we had learned from them; to move silently. Our soldiers had long since discarded their heavy leather boots with heels of oak tipped with iron and jingling straps at the ankle and knee and wore thin moccasins of deerskin. Shod in this way the sensitive sole of the foot felt the ground before one trod.

After half an hour of careful movement we reached a sharp turn in the avenue and came suddenly within sight of the encampment. It was quite clear in the moonlight; forty huts or perhaps a few more contained within a palisade ten or twelve feet high. At this point Ottigny sent two men back to the river to fetch up the raiding party. If all had gone well and according to plan, they should by now have landed and moved up the first quarter mile of the avenue. Two others were sent off to make a circuit of the camp and the rest of us concealed ourselves and waited.

An interminable time passed. Slight noises in the undergrowth around us were magnified in our imagination until we thought we were surrounded by enemies. Half a dozen times I saw Bidon level his crossbow at some tiny noise in the bushes near him and then lower it again on recognizing the slither of a snake or the jerky scurrying of a mouse or a rat. There were sounds from inside the camp, but they were all reassuringly normal. A dog howled once and was silent on being cursed. A baby cried and was hushed. Somewhere close to the palisade a man snored loudly, turning and moaning in his sleep as if beset by nightmares; a man in a fever perhaps.

At last, after what seemed an age, the raiding party arrived close behind us. They too came silently, but we knew they were there in the way one does know. It is almost as if the composition of the air changes, becomes heavy and full of humanity, or perhaps it is simply that one hears breathing.

Ottigny rose and vanished into the darkness behind us. A moment or so later he came forward again, this time with Laudonniere, and together they went out of the shadow of the trees and across the open ground towards the part of the palisade closest to us. We waited, knowing our parts and watching for the signal.

When the two men reached the wooden stockade one of them bent while the second climbed slowly on his back and then reached for the top. Slowly his hands slid up the rough wood, gripped the top and heaved. A head, shoulders, half a body appeared outlined against the pale sky, a leg was thrown over and there was Ottigny sitting astride the palisade like a boy about to rob an orchard, a perfect target in the moonlight.

Red breathed a single word in my ear. "Madman!"

I nodded. Mad, yes, but I envied the casual courage of the man.

Ottigny sat erect for as long as it takes to draw a breath and then disappeared, dropping down on the inside. That was the signal. We crouched, prepared to move, waiting for what was supposed to happen next. And almost immediately it came; a dull thump on the far side of the camp; the two men who had gone round the camp earlier had hurled a heavy rock or log at the side of the palisade. There was a sound of movement from inside the camp. Men's voices murmured and then called sharply; two or three dogs howled; there was a sound of soft running.

This was our moment. We rose and ran for the main gate of the camp, a little to the right and less than a hundred yards away. We reached it in a bunch at the same time as Laudonniere who had moved round under cover of the wall, and even as we reached it the gate swung loosely and began to open.

Ottigny was inside holding the heavy crossbar of the gate.

"Three guards awake," he said to Laudonniere. "They have all gone across to the far side to see about the noise."

Laudonniere nodded but did not answer. Nor did he look behind him. He ran on, straight across the center of the camp, clear and obvious in the moonlight, making for a low, oblong hut that stood somewhat by itself. Red, Arlac and two soldiers followed close on his heels, and the rest of us fanned out to make a sort of protective funnel across the center of the camp.

The raiders were still a few yards from the chief's hut when suddenly a figure rose from the ground by the doorway and took a couple of steps forward. I recognized the man straight away by his unusual height and build; he was Outina's personal bodyguard and was outstanding among the Indians for his size and immense strength. At this moment he held a short stabbing-spear in his hand and was raising it to strike when Laudonniere should come within range. But as he raised it Red, who had been running on Laudonniere's right and slightly behind him, put on a burst of speed and flung himself in a sort of dive straight at the giant. His head caught the man somewhere low down on the ribs and he went backwards with a coughing grunt like a wild boar with a spear in its throat. Laudonniere and Arlac plunged through the dark doorway without checking their pace.

It was all over before it had really begun. The raiders had hardly disappeared through the doorway before they were out again, running across the open, but not so fast now, carrying a heavy bundle between them; Outina himself, smothered in a skin robe, carried along by four running men, followed by a fifth.

We closed in after them as they went through the gateway. The camp was in an uproar with dogs howling, women screaming and men rushing about shouting at one another. For a while, however, the Indians seemed at a loss to know what had happened. We had moved too fast for them.

At the bend in the avenue we left a dozen men behind to cover the withdrawal against pursuit, but there was no pursuit. Halfway along the avenue we passed through the main party under La Caille drawn up along the shadow. Another unnecessary precaution. In a very short time the whole body of men was re-embarked in the shallops and we were floating once more in midstream, fifty or more yards from the end of the landing stage. Outina, with his hands bound behind his back, was set up in the middle of one of the boats, full in the moonlight. And there we waited for the pursuit to catch up with us.

We did not have long to wait. Soon we heard movements in the forest which sounded as if a large body of Indians was preparing to rush out of cover. The arquebusiers smiled grimly to themselves at this and blew on the ends of their matches in readiness for action. We had no need of them, however. Two men of the main party, while we advanced on the sleeping village, had systematically ripped great gashes in the sides of the numerous canoes drawn up on the beach.

Now, when the Indians suddenly plunged yelling from the cover of the trees and began to haul their canoes down to the water, their yells quickly turned to howls of rage or even cries of distress when they discovered the condition of their boats.

A few of them now threw themselves into the water and began to swim across the river towards us, but at a signal from Laudonniere one of the arquebusiers fired his piece at them. He had loaded with small shot which struck on the surface of the water with an angry hiss. The swimmers stopped immediately and returned towards the shore as fast as they could go.

Laudonniere now shouted to the shore. "Outina is our prisoner," he cried. "We shall not harm him in any way if you do as we command."

He waited for some answer from the Indians on the shore, but they stood in a sullen silence.

"When you have paid us enough corn, meat and beans to feed the men in our fort for six months," continued Laudonniere, "we shall release your chief to you."

Still there was no response from the Indians on the shore. The entire population of the village had now reached the river; men, women and children. They lined the bank and looked out towards our boats.

"We will wait here until sunset tomorrow," shouted Laudonniere finally. "If you do not bring what we ask by then I shall carry Outina down the river to our fort and keep him a prisoner."

No one moved among the Indians; they all stood and stared at us and at their chief as if they had been turned to wood. Then a piercing wailing sound rose in the air from one of the women. It was taken up by the rest and soon the whole forest seemed to be filled with the sad rising and falling notes. The women waved their arms wildly in the air as they wailed and swayed their bodies from side to side in time with the rhythm of their chant. The men stood still, as before, but looking down now at the ground.

Laudonniere turned angrily to Outina. "Why do they not answer me?" he demanded. "Why do they not return to their village for the food?"

"They do not believe you," said Outina, and it was clear from the tone of his voice that he did not believe either. "They think that you will take the corn and meat and beans and then kill me just the same."

"Perhaps they will believe tomorrow when they find us still here waiting," said Laudonniere.

Outina shrugged his shoulders expressively but said nothing. The wailing song of the women rose and fell monotonously and we were all filled with an unbearable melancholy.

8

Throughout the night more and more of Outina's people came down to the river bank and gazed across the water at their chief. The news of his capture must have spread to the surrounding villages which were also under his rule, for some thousands of Indians had gathered by the early hours of the morning.

Finally, a little before daybreak, they all drew back into the forest and left the river bank empty except for half a dozen old women who sat at the water's edge and kept up their wailing chant in thin, reedy voices. From time to time, as they sang, they shredded flower petals on the surface of the water.

We asked Outina the meaning of this little ceremony but he would only shake his head and mumble under his breath. He told us, however, that the six old women were witches whose particular business was the care of the dead, so we began to get a hint of what was going on in the Indians' minds.

We sat on in the boats, irritable, bitten by insects, hungry and rapidly losing hope. The sun rose and a clammy, unhealthy mist formed on the surface of the water for a while. Outina wrapped himself up in his blanket and appeared to be sleeping.

When the sun had risen above the tops of the trees we were suddenly startled by a great noise from the forest. It came from the direction of the village and moved quickly towards us. It seemed to consist of a banging of gongs, a shrilling of whistles and flutes and that same rhythmical chant sung now by many hundreds of voices. At first we thought the Indians had gathered in strength and were preparing to attack us. Laudonniere gave the order to raise anchors and be prepared for flight.

When the Indians emerged from the forest, however, they did so slowly and solemnly, walking in a long column out of the trees and along the river bank. None of them looked in our direction.

At the head of the column came four powerfully built men—one of them was Outina's son—carrying on their shoulders an Indian bed. It seemed to be loaded high with articles of clothing, weapons, pots and hunting gear. Behind this bed walked one woman, Outina's wife, with disheveled hair and torn clothing.

The column reached the edge of the water and halted. The chant rose higher and higher towards a hysterical climax and at this point the four men raised the bed from their shoulders and threw it out on to the river. At this the Indians gave a great wailing cry and then fell silent.

Laudonniere turned to Outina who was watching the proceedings with grim interest. "What is it?" he asked. "What are your people doing?"

For the first time since his capture Outina seemed to be slightly amused. He pointed at the bed, floating and turning slowly in the current, and said, "That is my funeral. My people have given me up for dead."

"I told them we should not harm you," said Laudonniere.

Outina shrugged.

Meanwhile the procession, silent now, was on the move again. The four men and the "widow" turned away from the river and disappeared into the forest. Behind them the rest of the tribe approached the edge of the water, a group of twenty or so at a time, hesitated and then followed the others into the forest. Garlands of flowers were cast on the river so that soon the waterlogged bed was surrounded by a great gay garden of blossom, all floating slowly down towards the sea.

In half an hour the last of the Indians had disappeared and the river bank was empty.

"What will happen next?" asked Laudonniere.

"Nothing," said Outina. "Nothing. They have gone home now. Tomorrow a new chief will be chosen."

"But this is ridiculous," raged Laudonniere. "They can see you. They know you are still alive. We are only asking for a payment of food..."

"Among our people," said Outina, "a captured chief is never allowed to return alive. To them I am already dead."

Here was a queer problem. A brilliant action brilliantly carried out and yet we were as far from seeing a sack of corn as ever we had been. Laudonniere seemed unable to solve it, and after a few more minutes' useless discussion with Outina he gave it up.

We returned slowly down the river, letting the current and the wind carry us for we were all too worn to row, and only stopped once—to recover some of Outina's more treasured possessions from the floating bed. He seemed pleased to get them, but was amazed that we should take the trouble.

9

Back at Fort Caroline the Indian chief was imprisoned in the hut originally used by La Croix and since the incident of the mutiny left unused. For two days more we waited for news to come from Outina's tribe. Laudonniere still thought, when the Indians heard that Outina was merely imprisoned and not dead, they would seek to buy his release. He ordered that Outina should be given daily exercise for an hour in the morning and an hour in the afternoon. The place chosen was outside the main gate of the fort and for part of the way along the causeway. He hoped that in this way Outina would be seen and his continued existence reported.

It was at this time that a messenger from Saturiba came secretly to see Laudonniere with an offer of much food in exchange for the old captive chief. Laudonniere refused to sell his prisoner of war. He knew that Saturiba hated Outina and would have sacrificed him to the tribal gods if he could have laid hands on him. This incident was kept secret and none but me in the fort knew of it. I was a party to some of the comings and goings of the messenger. But Laudonniere swore me to secrecy and until this moment I have kept my oath.

Very early on the morning of the third day of our return to the fort there was a great noise at the gate and very soon after a sentry brought a young Indian to Laudonniere.

"Silly young fool," the sentry was still grumbling. "Near as anything got himself shot. Wouldn't wait till I'd got a relief for my post . . . can't understand a word of his jabber, neither."

Laudonniere soothed the ruffled sentry and sent him back to his post on the gate and then set about trying to discover what the young Indian wanted. It was, in fact, Outina's youngest son, a boy of eleven or twelve. He was in a bad state; exhausted and nearly hysterical, so that it was some time before Laudonniere could get any sense out of him. Eventually it appeared that he had come to see his father and ask his advice. After we had kidnaped the chief and the people of the village had given Outina up for dead, they had been in the throes of a small-scale revolution. Among these Indians the chieftainship is not necessarily hereditary, and although the son of a dead chief is often chosen to take over the leadership, this need not happen and sometimes does not.

In this particular case a meeting of the old men had been held to decide on the next chief, and the old men had failed to agree. Some of them had voted for Outina's wife to act as regent until the younger son was old enough to be made chief, others voted that the oldest son should become chief immediately, and yet a third party voted for a distant cousin of Outina, a wealthy man who was suspected of having bribed some of the old men before the meeting.

In any case the meeting broke up without any agreement having been reached and the tribe was now in a state of unrest—almost of civil war. Outina's oldest son had been attacked by some enthusiastic supporters of the distant cousin, and from this a running fight had developed in which three or four people had been killed and many wounded.

Laudonniere pondered on this for some time and then had Outina brought across. The old chief came in with great dignity, refused the chair that was offered him and listened silently to his son's story. His expression did not change during the rather long recital and I began to wonder if he were really listening. But when the boy had finished, Outina turned slowly to Laudonniere.

"I must go back to my people," he said.

"And we must starve," said Laudonniere.

Outina shook his head. "I will see that you are sent the food you ask for," he said solemnly. "Even if my people are not grateful that my life has been saved, I am. I will pay for that life. But you must trust me."

Laudonniere thought for a moment. "We have no choice in the matter," he said at last. "Swear to me your most sacred oath that you will keep your word, and I will release you. The corn, however, must be delivered immediately. We can hardly wait another day."

10

The entire population of the fort, or at least those capable of staggering down to the strand and embarking, went with Outina to see him restored to his people. A warning was sent on before in the hope that the Indians would be ready with gifts when we arrived. And in fact they were. Some hundred or so of them lined the bank of the stream, each holding in outstretched hands a small gift of bread or beans or fish.

Outina landed with great dignity and was carried towards his village on the shoulders of his people. We poor hungry settlers were more interested in the gifts of food which the Indians left behind for us on the bank. We fell over one another to disembark and get at the food. Fortunately there was enough to satisfy our immediate hunger or there might well have been quarreling and fighting over the fragments. None of us had eaten a full meal for weeks and the effect of this little feast was to send most of the settlers off to sleep. Half an hour after we had landed Outina the river bank was strewn with prostrate men, sleeping carelessly, sprawled anyhow, with quaint smiles of satisfaction on their lean faces and perspiration bursting from them and soaking their hair and clothes.

Laudonniere and Ottigny had eaten sparingly and were prowling up and down the river bank, complaining of the danger and trying to stir a few men into wakefulness. Had the Indians been intending to attack us they could hardly have hit upon a better way of first making us defenceless. Twenty Indian braves, leaping out of the forest at that moment could have wiped out the whole settlement.

However, the Indians did not attack, and an hour or so later as the heat of the sun grew less the men began to stir, groaning with discomfort, holding their aching heads and feeling violently thirsty. Laudonniere and Ottigny nagged and bullied them into activity, and finally a camp was set up, fires were lit and a system of sentries organized. As evening fell Laudonniere judged that the Indians would have had time to collect the corn and other supplies promised by Outina, and he instructed Ottigny and Arlac to take a party of thirty arquebusiers up to the village to receive the stores. He attached Red and me to them as runners.

Ottigny gave the men time to make torches, to clean and load their weapons and to put themselves in order and then marched us off up the long avenue towards the village. We went cheerfully, happy in having full stomachs and with new hopes for the future.

The villagers seemed to be expecting us, for we were led immediately to the large central hut or council chamber and told that if we would wait there we should soon be satisfied. This hall, in fact an immensely large native hut with no windows and only one small doorway, was very gloomy. Even when our eyes had become accustomed to the dark we were not able to see more than halfway across it. When we first went in, there seemed to be a meeting taking place. Many old men were gathered at one end of the hall talking softly together. They turned and watched us as we took possession of the far end of the hut, and then went on with their meeting with rather more vigor. From the way in which one speaker after another waved his hands in our direction we assumed that they were talking about us. No doubt they were deciding how Outina's ransom was to be raised. Outina himself was not there.

After a very long wait three Indian women came into the hut, each carrying a sack of corn which was dropped quickly on the floor near us. The women then ran off giggling. Red opened the mouth of one of the sacks and felt inside.

"Maize," he said. "That's a start, anyway."

But it turned out to be a very slow start. Nothing more arrived for at least an hour and then a small boy came in with two small bags of beans, dropped them just inside the door and ran for his life.

Meanwhile there had been a certain amount of movement inside the hut. We had thought at first that this was part of the meeting; that some of the old men had been leaving and others coming in. Now, suddenly, we heard the unmistakable clink of weapons—a spear tapped against a shield, and the metallic ring was like a sudden warning.

Ottigny quietly told one of the men to light his torch, and when this was done we saw in the smoky light that some twenty or more armed warriors had come into the hut and were standing at the far end. They were in full war paint with daubs of white clay on their faces and in their hair. They were standing in a long line against the wall of the hut, most of them leaning forward a little, staring at us. They held their spears loosely and a little behind them, very nearly in the position for throwing them.

For a few seconds we all stood like statues, staring at one another down the length of the hut. The torch flickered and smoked so that for us the faces of the Indians seemed to be cast into a series of hideous grimaces. No one moved until Arlac, who was standing just beside me, shifted his arquebus to a more convenient and comfortable position, and this tiny action seemed to break the spell. The Indians shuffled their feet, turned their heads aside to glance at one another and then moved slowly into groups, some of them turning their backs on us as if to show that they had no interest in what we were doing.

The torch began to burn low, and before it went out each of our arquebusiers took a new match—that is, thick string soaked in saltpeter—from his pouch and lit it at the torch flame. Then, as the light died, each man stood vigilantly facing the Indians, ears straining for the least sound that might give warning of an attack, breathing gently on the smoldering end of his match so as to be sure it would not fail him in an emergency.

Then followed a weary time. We dared not relax, in case the Indians were in fact planning to attack us. Yet from time to time more sacks of corn were brought into the hut, so that it seemed as if the Indians really did intend to pay the ransom. But these sacks arrived at such long intervals that we also had cause to doubt whether we should ever get the full number that had been agreed on by Outina.

At last Ottigny lost patience. Picking half a dozen men to accompany him he left the hut and was gone for some time. During his absence we could hear that continuous sound of movement outside, and that occasional metallic clink that told of armed men. There seemed to be no doubt that we were slowly being surrounded by the native army. The slow arrival of the corn was probably a device to keep us there while armed tribesmen were called in from the more distant parts of Outina's kingdom. We had begun to believe that Outina himself had played us false when Ottigny hurriedly returned.

"We are in a fine trap," he said immediately. "The whole village is full of armed men, creeping about among the huts. Outina is being kept a prisoner by his own people and he can do nothing. The old man would keep faith with us if he could, but he is helpless. And see what I stumbled upon in the doorway of the hut!"

We had lit another torch in his absence and now by its light we saw that he held in his hand an Indian arrow.

"It was pushed into the earth," he said, "and you all know what that means."

"A declaration of war!" exclaimed Arlac. "How many of them are there?"

"How can one tell?" said Ottigny. "There might be ten thousand men hidden out there in the forest. But one thing is certain: every hour we delay here makes it worse for us. There seems to be no doubt that the whole tribe is gathering here, and that sooner or later they will fall on us. We cannot afford to wait any longer for a few sacks of corn. We must take what we have and get back to the boats—and even then we may have to fight to reach them."

So without more delay the order to march was given. The strongest of the men shouldered the sacks of corn, of which by this time there were eighteen or nineteen. Arlac with eight men went first, then two smaller parties who were to act as scouts on our flanks once we had got clear of the village, then the main party including those burdened with the sacks of corn.

To our surprise the village seemed deserted. We reached the main gate in the palisade without seeing a single Indian, and the gate was wide open. The moon had risen and we could see before us the long length of the avenue down which we must go. Ottigny halted us at the beginning of the avenue.

"Listen, men," he said quietly. "It seems to me the Indians have planned something against us, and for the moment we can't tell what it is. They are strong enough to have gone down river and seized the fort in our absence, but somehow I don't think that is it. They may have attacked the party we left at the river and destroyed the boats. They may be setting an ambush for us somewhere along this very avenue, knowing that it lies on our way home. But whatever it is, we must be ready for them. If we have to fight now it will be to the finish. We may not have time even to carry off our wounded, and I don't doubt that before morning comes some of us will be dead. . . ."

He paused and stared around at the starved faces of the army of scarecrows that he commanded, and strangely enough the sight seemed to encourage him.

"Whatever happens," he cried, "we shall be ready. And what's more, we will fight our way through it!" Then he gave a fierce tug at his equipment and in a hoarse voice ordered us on again.

Arlac and his eight men went fifty yards or so ahead of the main party and the two flanking parties disappeared into the black forest of either side. We could hear them from time to time breaking a way through the undergrowth. In this order, slowly and with every nerve of our bodies alert for the first hint of an attack, we moved up the avenue. Everything was silent now with the heavy, sulky silence of a great forest.

"Arlac is reaching the bend in the avenue," whispered Red to me. "Now is the danger point. In a few seconds he will be out of sight."

But the Indians were not such clever fighters as Red imagined. At the very moment he was saying this, there came suddenly a series of bloodcurdling yells and screams from the forest ahead of us; animal sounds they seemed for the most part, the cries of owls and cougars and wolves all mingling in a hysterical chorus. At the same time we saw Arlac and his men stop and form a small circle in the middle of the avenue. Then came the first muzzle flash from Arlac's own arquebus and the sound of the explosion was echoed hollowly down the rows of trees.

"Forward!" cried Ottigny. "They have sprung the trap!" and without waiting to see that his orders were being obeyed he began to run at full speed down the track. We followed close behind him.

As we began to run we saw the Indians break from cover and attack the small party. There must have been two or three hundred of them, screaming their war cry, waving spears and closing in relentlessly. We saw one man go down with a spear in his chest and this added new and furious energy to us all. We charged in for the last few yards yelling ourselves and with our swords swinging into the air and flashing in the moonlight.

The Indians were taken by surprise. They stood to receive the first shock of our charge but we did so much damage among them that they drew off into the forest immediately and we were left in triumphant possession of the avenue.

Our seemingly easy success made Ottigny thoughtful, however. "Only three hundred?" he was saying to Arlac. "Where are the others? Perhaps the main body is waiting at the river for us!"

In any case he decided to take no unnecessary risks and two scouts were sent forward to the river to see if it was safe for us to continue our march to the boats.

They were only gone a short time. A very large party of Indians were gathered together on the bank of the river, they said, and there was no sign whatever of Laudonniere and the men who had been left there. And no sign of the boats either.

We kept a grim silence at this news. No one dared to say what he thought. It was only too obvious that the main Indian army had wiped out the river party and sunk the boats. We were a very long way from the fort and hardly strong enough to make the distance on foot. It was better to say nothing and merely to wait for orders.

Ottigny and Arlac went a little apart from us and discussed the situation in low tones. When they returned Ottigny explained that we were to try to find our way across country, traveling as far as we could guess in a line parallel to the river. No one commented on this and we filed off through the trees, glad to be off the exposed avenue.

We marched all the rest of the hours of darkness and then rested for a short while when the sun rose. Ottigny was anxious to press on, however, and soon had us on our feet again. We had seen no sign of Indians since the ambush and we were beginning to feel we had outwitted them.

The forest was beginning to open out. By the middle of the day we had reached a part where we could see clearly for a mile or more in any direction. The chances of a sudden attack were now much fewer and we marched more at our ease, though we were all sinking with weariness. Finally, when the sun was at its hottest Ottigny called a halt. He chose a place sheltered by half a dozen tall trees, but surrounded by open park land. He placed two sentries in the branches of a tree and said the rest of us might sleep for an hour or so. We did not need to be told twice.

11

We were roused again when the sun was halfway down the sky. Arlac, apparently tireless, had been exploring the district while we slept and had discovered a fresh stream flowing strongly to the south. He said he believed we could not be far from the river.

After we had made a quick meal on a couple of handfuls of parched corn, we continued our march in a southerly direction, reaching the little stream a short while after. Ottigny decided to follow its course to the river and so continue along the bank until we came to Fort Caroline. By now we had almost forgotten about the hostile Indians and were more concerned with the distance still to go before we reached home.

So it happened that we tramped on through the high grass of that part of the country, laughing and chatting, greatly freshened by our sleep and strengthened by the food we had lately eaten, and walked straight into an Indian ambush.

Suddenly the calm and peaceful riverside scene was changed into a shouting, screaming pandemonium. Painted Indians leaped up out of the grass all around us and discharged a shower of flint-tipped arrows among us. With howls and screams they rushed in from all sides, to come, I suppose within range of their throwing spears. Had they closed right in on us I don't doubt that we should have been wiped out in a few minutes, but this they did not do. Although there were at least five hundred of them, and although they outnumbered us by almost ten to one, yet when they had formed a loose ring around us they began to circle, still screaming and waving their spears, trying to work up their courage perhaps for the final assault.

Without waiting for orders from Ottigny we had formed into a tight circle, all facing outwards. The arquebusiers dropped to their knees to get a steadier aim with their weapons and began to fire as calmly as if they were at a target practice. Those of us armed only with swords stood by them, ready should the Indians launch an attack, but meanwhile helping the soldiers to load.

When twenty or more Indians had been brought down by the expert shooting of the arquebusiers the enemy seemed to be growing doubtful. They widened their circle, trying to get out of range, and then suddenly, at some signal we did not notice, all disappeared into the long grass.

That was the worst time of all. The plain was strangely silent and empty, and yet, with the chill feeling in the spine, each of us knew that the Indians were drawing nearer and nearer in the grass. There was no escape from them in any direction.

One of the younger soldiers suddenly threw down his arquebus and began to laugh hysterically. "Look!" he cried. "Look! There are the boats, sailing in the grass! We shan't have to walk home after all; the boats have come for us!"

"Pick up your weapon!" shouted Ottigny sternly, trying to bring the man to his senses.

But the man took no notice. He put his hands to his mouth and shouted, "Ahoy, there! Ahoy!" and then began to run forward out of the circle towards a distant clump of trees.

"He thinks the trees are sails," exclaimed Arlac.

"Come back, you fool!" shouted Ottigny as the man went rushing forward into the long grass.

"Ahoy!" shouted the man again. "Wait—" The cry turned to a choking cough and he spun around and fell. We had time to see the Indian arrow in his throat before he disappeared in the grass.

We looked at each other in consternation and saw nervously to our weapons, ready for the attack we felt must come soon. And then, ever so faintly on the air, came a cry: "Ahoy! Ahoy!"

"It *is* a boat!" cried Arlac pointing. We followed the

direction of his finger in time to see the two familiar brown sails of our shallops emerge from behind a clump of trees and begin to move steadily across the waving grass of the plain.

Clearly Laudonniere and the main party had managed to embark and slip away down the river before the Indian war party reached them. They had probably given us up for lost when the sounds of the battle in the avenue had not been followed by our arrival at the landing stage.

"The river!" shouted Ottigny. "We have reached it without knowing." And then quickly, "It's our only chance. We must try to break through the circle. If we act quickly we may take them by surprise."

The arquebusiers calmly reversed their weapons, holding them like clubs. Some of them smiled faintly at one another as if this were some old trick they had been keeping up their sleeves till now.

"Lieutenant Arlac! Be so good as to take the rear with your party," said Ottigny.

"Sir!"

"Advance—at the double!"

We did take the Indians by surprise and were through the ring and beyond it before they had recovered. But they were lightly armed and fast-moving and they knew the country better than we. Three times we were forced to turn our backs on the brown sails and fight desperately as the Indians rushed us from the rear. Now they had the advantage, for we presented easy targets for their archers. Man after man was wounded, but struggled desperately on. The nearer we approached to the river the slower we were, either wounded ourselves or else helping a wounded comrade along. I myself had a small flesh wound in the right arm, and an arrow in my back that burned like fire. I could not draw it out for it was in too awkward a position. All of us drew courage from the sight of Ottigny who strode along with no less than seven arrows sticking out of his leather jerkin.

Somehow we dragged ourselves to the edge of the river where it merged into the plain through an area of marsh and waterlogged grass. The boats stood in midstream, some fifty or sixty yards off still. The leading men plunged in, thigh deep in mud, regardless of the danger of alligators and water snakes, and at the same time there came a thunderous volley from the boats as they opened fire on our pursuers.

We waded and swam, under the cover of this fire, and somehow we were given enough strength to reach the boats where we were hauled one by one to safety. Arlac and Ottigny were the last on the bank. They stood there, facing the enemy, like the Romans in the famous story, until the last soldier had struggled to one of the boats, and then they too turned and plunged into the river.

When they were finally hauled aboard each of these two brave officers were clutching a sack of corn. Two men had been killed and twenty-two seriously wounded for two bags of parched corn. If you like to see irony in situations, there is a fine example for you!

Chapter Seven

THE END

During the following fortnight five men died. The surgeon gave it out that they had died of their wounds and from loss of blood but a man makes new blood and wounds heal if the man is fed and cared for. There was no food in the fort and these deaths were, we knew, as much from starvation as from wounds.

As if to prove it the sixth man to die had not been wounded. He was an elderly settler who had remained behind at the fort during the raid on Outina's village. He had no fever.

Laudonniere called a meeting the following morning and announced that there was only one course left for us:

we must try to return to France. He knew, he said, that our ships were in poor condition. We had only the *Breton,* which had been rotting in the river since we first landed and leaked like a sieve, and the small brigantine that Fourneaux and his mutineers had returned in. The conditions of the voyage would be appalling and there were no food stores for the journey. Many of us, he said, would die before reaching France.

"Because of that," he added, "I shall give no orders in the matter. Those that wish to try the journey may do so. If any choose to remain here at Fort Caroline I shall stay behind with them as their leader and as the appointed governor of the colony."

There was hardly any discussion; everyone present chose to go with the ships. The sailing date was set for ten days thereafter, by which time the fort was to be dismantled and the settlers who lived outside the fort were to be warned. Red and I undertook to take one of the shallops up river to try to find Pierre Gambi; La Pouce promised to bring in the four or five farmers still out on the north bank of the river. The *Breton* was to be caulked and made as seaworthy as possible in the time and anchored in the mouth of the river ready for sailing.

2

Red and I set off that afternoon. We took no stores for the journey for there were no stores to be had. The wind was with us, and for two days and nights we made good speed up the river, living on shellfish and two lizardlike creatures that Red was lucky enough to shoot with the crossbow. The flavor was revolting and the flesh soft and formless but we were too hungry to care.

By midday of the second day we sighted a small island in the middle of the river. A small column of smoke rose among the bushes and low trees. We would have passed it, not daring to face an Indian party in our weakened condition. Indeed we were just leaving it astern when I noticed that only one small canoe was beached on the westward end of the island.

"A fire means food," said Red, "and there cannot be more than two or three of them."

We went about, dropped anchor in shallow water just off the flat muddy beach and splashed ashore. The Indian crouching over the fire at his cooking was taken by surprise. No doubt he had seen our sail passing but had thought we had gone on up river.

He was a very ugly fellow, short and squat with bowed legs and coarse, thickened features. He stood by his fire watching us, his arms dangling and his head turning from side to side as if he were considering escape.

"I wonder if there are some others hiding in the bushes?" said Red quietly.

To our surprise the Indian spoke out in French. It was uncouth French, spoken too far back in the throat and badly mangled, but we could understand it.

"No other. Me alone," said the Indian. He spoke quite violently as if he wanted to force us to believe him.

"Are we far from Edelano?" I asked.

The Indian started at the word and backed round the fire so that it was between him and us. "What you want Edelano?" he said frowning.

"We want to see Pierre Gambi," I said, and then thinking that the name would mean nothing to him, started to explain.

"Me know Gambi," said the Indian quickly. "Him friend. Teach me speak many words..."

Red laughed. "But of course," he said. "We might have guessed. Where else would an Indian learn French. Don't you recognize the true Parisian accent?"

The Indian relaxed when he saw us laughing. "Very good friend," he boasted. "Him master. Old man die. Gambi him chief Edelano."

Stranger things have happened. Pierre had told us that he was the old chief's son-in-law. Now apparently he had succeeded to the chieftainship.

The Indian seemed anxious to please us now. He offered us some of the food he had been cooking and when we had gratefully eaten it he escorted us back to the beach and told us the way we must take to reach Pierre's island before nightfall. It was not very far.

Just as we were preparing to go, however, Red glanced carelessly at the Indian canoe a few yards along the beach. Something about it attracted his attention and he went over to examine it more carefully.

"Alligator skins," he cried to me. "I thought Pierre said only the chief could own alligator skins?"

The Indian interrupted garrulously, explaining that the skins did indeed belong to the chief but that he was taking them down to the fort for him. "Chief he very busy man," he kept insisting.

It seemed to make sense, so finally we re-embarked and sailed off in the direction the Indian had indicated. The island of Edelano was even closer than he had said, and we reached it well before sunset. We could not sail up to it, though, for it was set back some distance from the river itself, in the center of a half-submerged marsh. Only an Indian canoe with shallow draught could reach it.

We waited, anchored as close in as possible, thinking that our presence would be reported to Pierre and that he would come out to us when he recognized the fort's shallop. The island was about a quarter of a mile off. We could see occasional movement of people between the huts that were clustered on one side of the island, and there were a number of canoes drawn up in a row above the water, but no one put out to us for a long time.

There was nothing we could do to reach the island so we waited as patiently as we could, inwardly cursing Pierre for his bad manners. Finally, however, just as the sun was setting, a slight figure moved down from the huts, pushed a canoe onto the water and began to paddle towards us. The marshes were obviously a good protection; the canoe wound about on a twisting course, sometimes seeming to go quite away from us. The light failed as it approached so that we could no longer make out any detail. Red hailed the canoe once, announcing us, but received no answer.

Eventually the canoe came close enough for us to see that its occupant was not Pierre Gambi at all but an Indian girl with small, attractive features and long braids of hair that fell down over either shoulder and almost reached her knees. She stopped paddling when she was within a few yards of us and said quietly, in a French that was indistinguishable from Pierre's own:

"Will you take me with you back to the fort?"

"Take you to the fort?" said Red, surprised. "But why? We want to speak to Pierre Gambi—to the chief."

"He is not here," the Indian girl said. "He went back to his people four days ago. You know. You are trying to trick me."

"We have not seen him," said Red. "We saw his servant taking alligator skins to the fort, but we've not seen Pierre."

The girl stared at us for a few moments, seeming not to understand. "His servant?" she said. "Pierre went alone—with the skins. There was a revolt. My people were angry because of the heavy taxes Pierre made them pay when he became chief. And if they complained he had them beaten. So they planned to kill him one night while he slept, only I warned him in time and he slipped away . . . he would not take me with him."

As she said this I realized that this girl must be Pierre's Indian wife of whom he had told us. I felt sorry for her but did not know what to say.

"We could take you to the fort," said Red. "Perhaps Pierre has got there by now."

While he spoke the girl was staring in a puzzled fashion as if trying to work something out. Now she interrupted Red. "What was this man like? The servant you spoke of?"

I described him as best I could.

"Thalina!" she exclaimed immediately. "He wishes to marry me and be chief. He followed Pierre the next morning. . . ."

She did not finish but picked up the paddle from the bottom of her canoe and dipping it deep in the water spun abruptly round with her back to us.

"But you are coming with us," cried Red.

"There is no need now," she said quietly over her shoulder. "Thalina has killed Pierre as he swore he would ... otherwise how would he have got the skins? Pierre is dead and ..." she paused a moment seeming weary and defeated and then she sat straighter and added proudly, "and I will go back to my people, where I belong."

We watched her as she paddled back towards the island, but she did not turn round again.

3

"There is not much doubt, I suppose," said Red some time later. "Little Pierre Gambi is dead."

"Should we try to avenge his murder?" I asked doubtfully. "This Thalina ... the man we saw ... he cannot be far ..."

But Red shook his head slowly. "Gambi's death will be avenged before very long," he said, "and without our taking any part in it."

"I don't understand," I said.

"We are going away," said Red, "but others will land here and try again to make a colony. Next time they will come in greater numbers and with more guns ... and their greed for gold will be greater. I don't think the Indians will have much of a chance against them."

"The colonists could live alongside the Indians in peace, just as you planned on the farm," I said.

"They could," said Red. "But do you honestly think they will?"

4

We arrived back at the fort with two or three days to spare and found it deserted. The main gate hung open to the causeway, and a cloud of bright birds flew up in a scare as we walked through.

"We have been left behind!" I cried in a panic.

"Perhaps they are at the ships," said Red sensibly. "They would wait till the sailing date. Surely they would wait."

We went down the river towards the sea in a torture of anticipation, fearing the moment when we should come out from the last bend and look down the last straight stretch of water to the mouth—and find it empty.

But it was not empty, and I saw the first sail. We grinned at each other like fools, feeling quite sick with relief.

"We could have managed," said Red, but without any great conviction.

And then we saw there were six ships at the mouth of the river instead of two. Four of them were standing out to sea with sails furled, big trim ships, gleaming black and white like ships in a dream.

"Spaniards!" I exclaimed.

"Nonsense," said Red sharply. "You never saw a Spanish vessel as spick and span as those are. I'll stake anything they're English."

5

So my story comes to an end. Red was right, of course. The four ships at the mouth of the river were under the command of the English sailor Sir John Hawkins. They had been selling slaves farther south in the Spanish colonies, and leaving Cuba suddenly on account of a fight between English and Spanish seamen they had sailed with half-empty water casks. Hawkins had put in to the River of May to charge his casks before returning to England.

The rest must be well known. Sir John Hawkins sold us a good ship—the *Swallow* it was called—and provisions for the voyage home. As I write these words men and stores are being transferred to the *Swallow* and tomorrow, given a fair wind, we shall be on our way homeward.

True, we are not very certain of our reception there, and many of the settlers are returning a good deal poorer than they were when they left. Red and I go back rich in experience only. Red has a small bag of maize hidden in his kit; he hopes to try it out on French soil. I shall go with him.

As I wrote those words Red appeared at my shoulder. "Make an end of it, Pierre," he said. "The wind is changing; there is no more time for scribbling."

As usual he is right; I shall do as he says.

HISTORICAL NOTE

THE STORY told here is substantially true. Even the names of the people involved are the names of real people, and all the incidents of importance are accounts of real incidents.

On the other hand this is a novel and not a history book. I have taken considerable liberties with the known personalities and I have invented almost all the conversation. The only speech that is vouched for, word for word, is the address La Caille makes to Laudonniere on the occasion of the mutiny, and even this is taken from an account written many years after the event.

For those interested in sources this is where my information came from:

There are three main original sources for a description of the events that took place in Florida. (1) The letters of Réné de Laudonniere, (2) an account by Jacques Le Moyne, and (3) a story of the colony by the carpenter Challeux.

All three are summarized and made into one continuous tale in *The Pioneers of France in the New World* by Francis Parkman, Chapters, 4, 5 and 6.

Jacques Le Moyne made some beautiful drawings of typical incidents of Indian life. These were engraved by De Bry and are often reproduced in history books dealing with the period. The whole forty-eight drawings are reproduced at the original size in a book called *America: The New World,* edited by Stefan Lorant. An English artist, John White, also did a few drawings of the Indians of Florida of a slightly later period. The originals of these drawings are in the Print Room of the British Museum.

In *Adventures in the Wilderness,* edited by Winter, Skinner and Wood, Volume 1 of a large work called *The Pageant of America,* published in England by Humphrey Milford, there are many reproductions of drawings by Le Moyne, White and others, and these are all very interesting.